I0578096

A NOTE ON THE AUTHOR

Hugo Grylls was born in London in the last millennium.

He was immersed in the waters of Eng Lit for as long as he could hold his breath by his parents, but they held him by his heels, so while most of this little Achilles got (and remains) wet, his most vulnerable spot was never touched.

The only axiom that has influenced Grylls is Montherlant's: "It is when you wish for nothing that you will become the reflection of God." With that in mind he decided to hell with solvency, he'd try to eke out a living from his pen.

Hugo Grylls is currently *nel mezzo del cammin* (if Dante's actuarial skills are to be relied on). This is his life's work to date.

Book Ends

Hugo Grylls

WriteSideLeft
2020

ISBN: HB: 978-1-9162610-2-0
ISBN: TPB: 978-1-9162610-0-6
ISBN: eBook: 978-1-9162610-1-3

Compilation & Cover Design by S A Harrison

Published by WriteSideLeft UK
www.writesideleft.com

Book Ends

Hugo Grylls

"Des services! des talents! du mérite! bah! soyez d'une coterie."
Télémaque (v. Stendhal, *Le rouge et le noir*, ch. 57)

Crede quia impossibile est

Contents

Publisher's Note

We're on a risk here. Although all the characters portrayed in this book are fictitious, and any supposed resemblance between them and real persons, living or dead, is purely coincidental, the same cannot be claimed of the central element of the story which, as far-fetched as it may seem, is based sedulously on real events of the early 1990s, shortly before the Internet and e-mail.

Chapter One: Fast Track, Slow Track

"What areas have you been looking at?"

The truth was that Jacob Pursey hadn't been looking at anything much. But after his tutor told him he'd be lucky to get one degree, and that any attempt to put himself up for another would be hubris, he thought he'd better seek his future elsewhere.

Asked the kind of work he wanted, which was what this mealy-mouthed question amounted to, he had no real answer. To make matters worse, already at twenty-two he was as sure as you can be that he never would have one. He remembered how it had been when as a child people asked him what his favourite colour was. He didn't really have one of those either: nothing is a dish for every day, and while one might like green on, for example, the floral fuse through which the force gets driven in a poem by Dylan Thomas, one might not be so keen on it if, again for example, it were to manifest itself on the membrum virile. But he knew he had to say something. To colours, it was beige; to areas it was:

"Journalism, television, radio, advertising, publishing..."

He had a couple more on his list but at that point the careers adviser interrupted with:

"Publishing? Book publishing? Competitive. Very competitive.

I would recommend that you apply there only if you think of yourself as one of the top ten people of your year."

If you take a red rag like that and waggle it in the face of a young bull with a B.A. in the offing, more than a millilitre of testosterone and an admixture of faith that there is no better creature than he alive, what outcome would you expect other than that he immediately shelve his first four ideas and charge headlong at the quintessence?

§

"George Mascaret?"

"Hey, Jez. Good to hear you; how's every damn thing?"

"Mustn't grumble. How's it hanging with you?"

"By a thread, as usual; living and partly living."

A quotation and Jez Yaxley knew who from, or at least he thought he did. If he'd heard it on a telly quiz he'd have shouted at the screen like a goodun, but with this bloke he knew to exercise caution. He was reasonably sure it was T.S. Eliot but it could just about have been Tennyson or any other of those dying-fall whingers. If he was wrong he knew he'd be in for an "Oooh no Jez" and he wasn't in the mood. If he was right he'd get a "Good, but do you know where?" Which he didn't. So after a perfunctory "I know the feeling", he reverted to the script in front of him.

"Now, are you up for an exciting new challenge?"

"You bet; but never rained such showers at these without

thunderbolts in the tail of them. Whose throat must I cut?"

That one Jez didn't know and he had no interest in finding out. He thought literary banter, enough already.

"No throats, just prose. We've got this book on the history of English football. The images are wonderful – never before seen angles of famous matches, Alf Ramsey picking his nose, Beckham getting tattooed, Hillsborough, all amazing. But the text is shit. Would you look at it?"

"Of course."

"Good man. The answers to your next questions are two thousand pounds and Thursday week. Does that sound possible?"

"I'm a bit pushed at the moment: can you see your way to two and a half?"

A non-electronic hiss on the line: the caller sounding like he's punctured himself.

"The margins are very tight on this one. But as it's you, hold on while I double-check the costings."

A new noise, like that of documents being riffled, created by a flip from the showbiz section to the racing pages of *The Sun*.

"The budget's even smaller than I thought. I could go as high as two two-fifty, but the powers that be won't wear any more, I'm afraid."

Dramatic momentary pause, then:

"Very well, you're on."

"I knew I could count on you. I'll send the manuscript."

"We must do lunch."

"Yes, we really must. As soon as this one's out of the way, eh?"

Jez pressed the prong to clear the line, closed his left eye, stuck his tongue out of the right corner of his mouth and made wankers at the receiver on his shoulder.

§

Arriving well early for an interview at a once and future private residence in Bloomsbury Way, Jacob Pursey took up so much of the exiguous reception area for so long that the staff members who had to edge past him on their way to and from lunch grumbled about his presence to Gill Furneaux the managing director, but she, unwilling to let the counsel of underlings prevail in any matter, left him there until the appointed hour. By then her Number Two, with whom she'd been discussing the important question of whether her husband suspected them, had gone off to take a phone call from his matrimonial solicitor. Her secretary was eating a sandwich in Bedford Square, so she had to fetch the applicant from downstairs herself.

Since Gill had only the vaguest notion of who this unwholesome-looking youth might be and what he had applied for, it being Number Two who was supposed to deal with that kind of thing, she covered herself according to time-honoured commercial principle by bombarding him with hostile questions.

Looking sneerily at his CV: "It says here you got 'Class two (Roman numerals) Honours'. I take it that means a two-two."

Pursey replied that his university didn't make a distinction and that he had got an upper second. This was not even partly true.

"What does your father do?"

Pursey, as yet unaware that the correct answer to this is "It's all right, thanks, he's got a job", told her that his parents owned a property firm. He didn't add that the full extent of its holdings was a little shop on the ground floor of the family residence; neither did he mention that it was empty more often than it was let as a hardware store, its designated purpose.

And then the clincher: "Why should we offer you this post?"

Pursey was drawing breath – not that he'd thought of anything to say – when the door opened.

"So sorry I'm late."

"This is Baxter Stratton, marketing director."

Pause for handshake and a moment of general sight-reading as new arrival and interviewee primafacied each other. The former had some idea of what he was looking at but little interest; the latter had no conception of what a marketing director was, did or was meant to do but thought the gadge looked smooth and dangerous in possibly equal measure and found it a heady mixture. Apart from the teeth, which reminded him for an irreverent moment of those put in by Barry Humphries when he appeared on stage as Australian Cultural Attaché Sir Les Patterson.

Gill Furneaux said: "I'm now going to ask you all the same things again, in the same order, firstly so that Baxter can catch up and secondly to see if you've got the brains to give the same answers twice."

The sometimes overlooked benefit of walking on hot coals is that it warms the feet. By the time the interrogator returned to the unanswered question, Pursey had the feeling public speakers sometimes get that they could go on longer. But whereas orators usually conceive this notion after they've sat down and it's too late, Pursey was still well placed to show that he'd started to get the hang of it.

"I accept that I have no direct relevant experience, this would be my first job, but the trouble with experience is that it restricts, creates blinkered thinking. I will bring a fresh pair of eyes to your publicity department because I'm highly educated and have seen your advertising material from the consumer's perspective. I won't have to guess what book buyers want, because I am a book buyer and I know. A person who has a reliable sense of what will sell, someone who can achieve sales within strict budgetary constraints, is one who can make a major contribution to this company. And I am that person."

As he spoke he could scarcely believe that such words were issuing from him but he would recall them with accretions of pride in, above all, the way he avoided the elementary mistake of using the conditional mood. No "I think I cans" or "I hope I might one day be able to's", just categorical assertion, passim: I will, I won't, I am.

And when he'd finished he saw that his interlocutors were no longer captains of industry; they were gloops watching the skies as a new planet swam into their ken.

§

The football book turned out to be no ordinary shit but the kind of shit that brings shit into disrepute. It was in its way a tour de force. If a sentence began with "In addition" you could rely on it also to contain "also" and not infrequently "as well" too. The author displayed a mastery of cliché that enabled him dependably to bypass good idiom and opt unerringly for any word or phrase desiccated of meaning through overuse. Most Scots were dour and those who weren't were canny; uncertainty was glorious; black players had silky skills; custodian was an elegant variation of goalkeeper; games of two halves concluded at the end of the day; limits were parameters; love affairs were torrid.

Perhaps to counterbalance his use of what he took to be demotic English as she is spoke, and to adduce evidence of a continental canvas, the author worked in numerous foreign words and phrases. And how he made them fit the subjects he was describing. Franz Beckenbauer didn't have plans, he had Weltanschauung. Eamon Dunphy and Johnny Giles never talked, they did the craic. Michel Platini wasn't elegant, he was chic in italics. Enzo Bearzot worried more than once about maintaining *la bella figura.*

Interspersed with this were metaphors, plenty of them, all ghastly, including on page one-three-five: "Much blood and sweat went into pulling the club up by its bootstraps because it was on the deck".

And numerous unrelated antecedents, possibly more than had ever previously been aggregated, stuff like:

"Charlie Nicholas signed for Arsenal in 1983. Four years later, having never delivered as hoped, they brought in Alan Smith to replace him".

George Mascaret was an editor, and untangling thickets like this is what editors are meant to do. He knew he'd struggle with the mind-reading passages, such as that in which the author asserted that "Brian Clough's egotism was but the shrunken residue of the all-embracing feeling that in the beginning coalesced self and universe". But he'd seen worse and he needed the money.

§

Jacob Pursey left home on his first day at work with his father's oft-rehearsed business precepts charactered in his memory. There were six of them. Although they'd never been officially numbered, Jacob always remembered them in the order:

one: work migrates to those who can do it;

two: never assume that anyone is not having an affair with anyone else;

three: never use analogy or reductio ad absurdum to illustrate a point;

four: never imagine that if you're good at menial tasks you'll be fast-tracked to the boardroom; he who shovels shit efficiently gets no other reward than more shit to shovel;

five: never low-rate yourself; people take you at your own evaluation (this sat uncomfortably beside his mother's favourite saying, "Self-praise is no recommendation", but in practice he used her axiom only when affecting modesty);

and six: if you must work late, make sure the boss sees you leave.

As soon as Pursey was installed in a small office that also contained Cath, new like him, and Ella Bethune, his immediate boss or, as he learned to describe her, "line manager", he was what Baxter Stratton called "tasked" to compile a new catalogue of all Volkmer & Iles' backlist titles. To this end he was given a big fat computer printout on green paper in a plastic binding that was hard to lift, harder to hold and impossible to open on his desk. He kept it on the floor next to his chair and leant down to refer to it, an action that enabled him also to check out Ella's legs; but Ella was dead professional and didn't flirt.

The list contained every book ever published by VI, as the firm was known; Pursey's job was to arrange them all alphabetically by category. For the most important titles he had to find blurbs or, in the absence thereof, to write new ones. If he didn't know anything about such books and the titles didn't make the contents clear, he was to talk to the editors who commissioned them.

But many of the relevant people were dead or gone, and those who remained adopted defensive postures that amounted to "What's it to you?" Some didn't remember the titles and had to look them up; others had joined the firm many years after the books were published and merely inherited them as part of their backlist. In numerous cases the original promotional material had been lost or discarded, so the only way to discover what the books were about was to look at them, but they were stored fifty miles outside London in some dormitory town and the cost of sending them to the office or Pursey to the warehouse was more than VI would bear.

So he had to use his initiative. Unaware of what *Westward Ho* by Dekker might be, he appended an exclamation mark and listed it under Geography. Never having heard of *When William Came* by Saki, he put it under Adult between *Urolagnia: The Coffee Table Book* and *Your Pain, My Pleasure*.

Everyone seemed pleased with the finished list and Ella offered to take Jacob out after work.

Their drink – in a pub frequented mainly by barristers who were louder and, from their clothing and the size of their rounds, richer than Pursey could ever hope to be – was followed by dinner at a trattoria in Sicilian Avenue. Pursey took the conversational lead throughout, skilfully maintaining as the theme interested but non-prurient questions about Ella's background, family and professional, while pumping her for information about the company.

He thus gathered that Max Volkmer and Harold Iles had set up the business after they'd been sacked from jobs in the City. They agreed that they were going to start off with quiz books, light blue novels and reprints of classics but their scheme almost foundered on a dispute about which of their names should come first. Iles wanted alphabetical order; Volkmer wanted euphony. Iles cited great combos that supported his point – husband and wife, Marks and Spencer, Harvard and Yale, Sacco and Vanzetti. Volkmer countered with mum and dad, Swan and Edgar, Oxford and Cambridge, David and Charles. Fearing impasse, they considered a few animals and birds, but the names of most fauna were already in use by publishers and those that weren't were either preposterous or too obviously derivative from those that were taken. Finally they made the sound decision. The victor was quietly triumphalist, the loser loquaciously resentful. Volkmer and Iles remained co-chairmen but seldom came to the office and saw each other even less frequently. In due course Iles went to sleep and retained only nominal involvement in the firm.

Absent from the dinner but requiring some discussion during its three courses was Cath. Ella hadn't much liked the upstart from the moment she told her that VI was merely a stepping-stone on her inexorable progress to taking over a rival publisher in which her father was the majority shareholder. Jacob had at first regarded Cath as competition. He was not attracted to her and after she had asked, on overhearing him on the phone to his own male parent, if Pursey père was "in trade", he despised her.

This background explains the following exchange:

Ella: "Cath's sweet, isn't she?"

Jacob: "Sweet, yes. And going places, I feel".

By the time the bill arrived, the talk had turned to literature. Once Jacob had got Ella off the life and work of Henrik Ibsen, the subject of her dissertation twenty years previously, she happened to mention first an author and then a book that he knew about although he hadn't read either. He seized both opportunities to expatiate.

Of Timothy Mo, he professed admiration for the "acute reckoning of the small change of human interaction", a phrase he'd picked up from a Sunday newspaper. Of *Zuleika Dobson* he said: "I'm not convinced that it's really, strictly a novel. It's a magnificent piece of writing", he added so as not to offend her, "but it doesn't develop as a novel should".

These judgments impressed Ella, who took him back to hers for coffee.

§

After wrestling with the first couple of chapters of the football book, George Mascaret turned his attention to speculative projects – ideas of his own that he from time to time submitted to publishers and magazine features editors. That they almost never accepted them did not mean his effort was entirely wasted – it reminded others that he was alive and available for selection. It was frequently the case that after he'd either been ignored or had the thanks-but-no-thanks he was offered a project of theirs. Whether their ideas were less fanciful than his own he had long ago decided not to think about too much.

He spent the morning putting the finishing touches to a couple of presentation spreads for a proposal called *Title Deeds*, which listed famous works named after quotations from other books. Based on the premise that there is no such thing as common knowledge, every entry spelt it all out. *Far from the Madding Crowd* (1874), a novel by Thomas Hardy (1840–1928), from a line in "Elegy Written in a Country Church Yard" by Thomas Gray (1716–71). *The Crying Game* (1992), a film directed by Neil Jordan starring Forest Whitaker, Miranda Richardson and Stephen Rea, from a 1964 hit single of the same name written by Geoff Stephens and sung by Dave Berry.

Friends remarked and family complained that none of his work was original; George agreed but defended it on the grounds that the arrangement of the material was new. "Besides", he would add, "it ain't stealin'".

Having mailed the pages to his established contacts, he received an article on astrology for inclusion in *Medieval Science and Superstition*, an encyclopedia that he was reading for a U.S. publisher. Written by a professor at the University of Novi Sad, the piece was lousy with what can only have been Serbian idioms rendered literally into English. Although Mascaret was accustomed to such material and liked to think a bit wishfully that he made the prose of random foreigners read like that of Joseph Conrad, there was one section of this work that defied interpretation: a paragraph in which readers were expected to believe that "The number of signs of the zodiac was fixed to correspond with the twelve orifices of the human body". Mascaret was about to put his pen through the whole section when he suddenly thought that, since this bloke was billed as the world's greatest living authority on the subject, there was a possibility that he knew what he was talking about. Having counted his own orifices and failed to arrive at the same total, Mascaret thought first about seeing a doctor and then, more seriously, about ignoring the problem and keeping his own counsel. Having concluded that it would be unprofessional to do nothing, he embarked on the course most dreaded by people in his line of work: he brought his query to the attention of the author.

§

When printed and distributed, Jacob Pursey's catalogue proved controversial. The sales representatives hated it because it led to them having to write down orders for books that hadn't been in print for a generation and would probably never be resuscitated. But the editors, having done little to assist in the preparation of the list, viewed the finished article in a charitable light: it showed VI's range and depth, and if any particular title accumulated sufficient dues it might be reissued in revised format, which would save them having to come up with new ideas. The reps blamed the catalogue on its compiler, who became known to them as Cy, an acronym of "callow youth". Pursey was thus drawn to the attention of Baxter Stratton, who had by now forgotten him and lived too much in the present to welcome reminders of the past.

§

George Mascaret rose before dawn and wrote in his Journal:

"Things I used to believe when I was young. One was that death came when you reached a philosophical conclusion that rendered life unsustainable".

He stopped to reflect on how much dimmer that made him than Matthew Arnold, whose "Growing Old", completed before the poet was twenty-seven, demonstrated a more precocious understanding of decay.

But reminding himself of the dictum "Write what you know", he returned to the page and added:

"Another was that if you were any good at anything you wouldn't need to blow your own trumpet, you'd be discovered".

He then killed time in the bath until he thought it was late enough for Wilby Bestsellers to be up and running. A little after eleven o'clock he phoned in his report on the football book:

"The author's not a natural writer."

Jez Yaxley told him that was the understatement of the century, if not what he called *the minellium.*

"I was being polite."

"Don't be."

"I can knock it around a bit, take out the worst excesses."

"Thing is, George, we were really looking for something rather more radical than that. I think what I'm basically asking is, Can you rewrite it?"

"I can," said George with a rising whine. Then he paused, hoping that Jez might fill the silence with an improved inducement or a revised deadline, but experience had taught him that he would get no change out of either pocket, so he just sighed and added: "I guess that's what I do."

Mascaret reflected on this exchange. Had he not been hired to edit the book? And was he not now about to become its unacknowledged author? And was he going to be paid no more for the latter than he had been offered for the former? He spent the rest of the day doodling, staring out of the window and trying and failing yet again to read Smollett's translation of *Don Quixote*. Playing on his calculator, he confirmed for the nth time that five-three-one-double seven-o-four, when viewed upside down, spells "Hollies". He then chanced to discover that this was his twenty thousandth day on Earth.

§

Baxter Stratton looked through the half-moons that he wore for effect at the annual review form completed by his current visitor, Ross Runnacles, VI sales manager.

According to the rap sheet, Runnacles had increased turnover in his section of the business by ten per cent in the previous financial year. In consideration thereof, he was now asking for an equivalent raise in pay.

Although Baxter pretended to be unprepared for the negotiating table, he had had a pre-meeting confab with Gill at which they agreed that Runnacles had a bloody nerve asking for anything and thrashed about in search of a non-confrontational way of turning him down.

After rehearsing some macroeconomic flatulence about soaring oil prices and the continuing instability of the South African market, Baxter had looked through the sales-by-customer printout and there made a significant discovery, which he now revealed in a minor coup de théâtre.

"Ross, I have to say that although these performance figures are undeniably good, it appears that all but about five kay of remainder sales are to a single outlet…"

Runnacles reddened; he knew what he'd done was risky, but under normal circumstances – if he'd kept quiet and never asked for more – he might have been right in his assumption that no one would have noticed the flaw in his master plan to own a better flat than anyone else at his level in the trade. It had worked well for two years, but now that they had checked the figures he saw plainly what was coming.

"… and I was surprised, to put it mildly, when I found that nine out of every ten overstock units are sold to an outlet in Bristol named Runnacles Bookends. I don't know if you know it."

Ross had considered calling the shop "Moonlighting", but he always liked his own name better than any other, a pride that was suddenly starting to look like hamartia. Still, he was a good sport; he folded his arms, leaned back in his chair and readied himself for the inevitable. Nothing in his work became him like the leaving it.

§

A week after George had Swiftaired a request for clarification, this arrived from Yugoslavia:

Dear Mr Mascaret

I think the problem may be the word "orifice", which means "opening".

I hope this helps.

Sincerely

Bosko Putnikovic

By return of post went:

Dear Professor Putnikovic

Thank you for your prompt reply.

I fear I may not have made my difficulty entirely clear. I am familiar with the word "orifice"; what I cannot manage is to identify more than seven or eight such places, to wit: two ears, two nostrils, one mouth, one urethra, one anus and (normally in women only) one vagina.

Please advise.

Best wishes

George Mascaret

§

In a day room at a Heathrow hotel, Gill and Baxter lay on the bed and mused about a replacement for Runnacles. They agreed the vacancy had to be filled quickly and cheaply. That ruled out advertising; the appointment would have to be internal.

Each of Baxter's suggestions inspired a sarcastic remark; each of Gill's brought an impersonation. The first name that failed to produce a hostile response did so only because they both struggled to put a face to it.

"Catalogue boy? Is he thrusting?"

"Depends what you mean. He shtupped Ella about as soon as he landed."

"He didn't? How do you know?"

"It's common knowledge. He tells people it was like 'Norwegian Wood', except that he didn't sleep in the bath. And you should see her go red every time his name gets mentioned." Baxter half-sang the last six words to something like the tune of "Me and Julio Down by the Schoolyard".

"Well I suppose if he can pull that…. You wonder why he'd want to, though."

"She's fine; a bit dull, but aren't they all? Nice chassis."

"You wouldn't, would you?"

"Dunno. Never say never."

"You haven't, have you?"

"Don't be ridiculous."

"I know you, Stratton, anything with a skirt and a pulse."

§

Dear Mr Mascaret

The twelve are: two eyes, two ears, two nostrils, two nipples, one umbilicus, one anus, one urethra and one vagina.

I trust all is now clear and look forward to seeing the complete edited version.

Sincerely

Bosko Putnikovic

George, having thus far denied himself an unrestrained response to the foreigner's presumption that he didn't know a common word in his native language, found this more than he could courteously abide.

"Putting aside what I should have thought was obvious, namely that the number of signs of the zodiac corresponds to – not 'with' – the number of months in the year, 'orifice' implies capacity for ingress as well as egress. What goes in to the nipples apart from rings, you Yug retard?"

But recalling Ecclesiastes' "A living dog is better than a dead lion", he wrote none of that down. He signed off the piece and returned it to Denver, Colorado content in the knowledge that he had done all he could. He wrote in his Journal:

"Adam and Eve didn't get expelled from the Garden of Eden. What happened was that they trusted God, but He didn't trust them so He hired the snake to snoop. Our first parents reached the conclusion that if that was how He was going to behave, they would defy Him by eating the forbidden fruit and then get the hell out of it; it must be better in the Land of Nod or wherever it was they went. And the poor old serpent carried the can and got kneecapped. Far from being lovesome things, gardens in the Bible are dangerous places – look what happened to J.C. in Gethsemane."

He then started again on the football book. Cutting the bad bits was easy. Indeed, it was almost a pleasure. He sometimes felt that he was being less than completely faithful to the author's intention, but more often he was unable to tell what that might have been, other than perhaps to fill space on the page. Much of the prose had a dream-like quality, not in the way of great lyrics by Shelley but in the way that makes sense only until you wake up and come to think about it, at which moment it evanesces like mist on a summer's morning. The few paragraphs that did not require major surgery he left untouched, not because they were any good, but because they were the thisness of the work.

§

A little under six months after Jacob Pursey joined VI, he was summoned by Baxter Stratton.

"We've kept a pretty close eye on your progress here and we really like the way you go about things. We'd like to move you closer to the engine room and make you our new sales manager."

Pursey's promotion had a purgative effect on Cath, who,

thinking not unreasonably that she was the more accurate copywriter and knowing that her dad had a job for her elsewhere, handed in her notice a week later. Ella, who had never previously slept with a colleague and would not have minded a return fixture, had been discouraged by Pursey's post-match froideur. Neither of them ever subsequently referred to their night together, and she noticed that he was much friendlier to women in the office with whom, as far as she could tell, he had not been so intimate. Full of doubt, Ella feared that she had made her move too quickly and thus created the impression that she was a manhunter. A moment later, she decided that she was a trollop or, if not, a woman who could forgivably be mistaken for one. On learning that Pursey was moving onwards and upwards she concluded that he had taken advantage of her. This fitted neatly with her view of herself as a perpetual bridesmaid and of nearly all her lovers as manipulative bastards. So having got what she thought she deserved she was satisfied and wished him well.

The VI representatives took the news like an enema. Cy consolidated his reputation among them as a worthless chancer at his first sales conference, where he sprayed the auditorium with some of the fundamental tenets of his rapidly coalescing philosophy of publishing.

Among the truths that he now held to be self-evident, but not so self-evident that they didn't need saying, was that the title of a book is very important.

"Take *Lord of the Flies* by William Golding. That book sold yay million copies worldwide so you can't exactly say it was a failure, but it still had a lousy title. What I mean is, you are probably well aware that it's another name for the Devil, but how can you expect ordinary people to know that? I guarantee that if we rather than Faber had been involved in the marketing of that book it would have had a better title and it would have sold twenty-seven per cent more copies across the board."

Sat at the back of the room, the rep for Ireland, the only freelance member of the sales force and hence, unlike the wage slaves, an independent spirit, asked "What would you have called it, then?" but he said it quietly, enabling Pursey, if he heard it, to ignore him.

Pursey's animadversions came after the opening remarks in which Gill and Baxter claimed that Volkmer & Iles was doing well notwithstanding the challenging economic climate (uncertainty in the Middle East, impending general election, the tottering Yen) and that the only obstacle preventing the company from overtaking Simon & Schuster as a publisher of world renown was the shortcomings of the sales force. There was then a break for coffee followed by a session devoted to the presentation of new books.

The editors came in turn and talked briefly about every title of theirs that was due to appear over the next six months. Although Pursey stayed silent throughout this phase of the proceedings, it was here that he first made his mark. The previous day, he had summoned all those slated to address the conference and forbidden them to refer to any competing products – a VI title was henceforth to be regarded as by definition sui generis. Thus when the reps asked "Are there any other books available on this subject?" they were told no; if they made comparisons with other publications they knew about – as when one of them likened *An Anthology of Hall Caine* to *Hall Caine: The Collected Works*, which had been produced by Heinemann the previous year – they were told that the rival books were not in the same class. Pursey further instructed the editors to respond to any questions about where in multi-department bookshops a particular title should be placed – Is *The Global Warming Primer* science or politics? – with the simple and invariable slogan "In the front window".

Pursey's closing address conjured the reps to redouble their efforts. His key message, "Be kings in your territory", was stated thrice, a tricolon inspired partly by a dim childhood recollection of the Lewis Carroll gag "What I tell you three times is true" and partly by a VI management handbook which stated that a trainer should always tell his pupils what he's going to tell them, tell them, and then tell them he's told them. Sitting on either side of their new young champion, Gill and Baxter looked like proud parents. On the way out, the Irishman said they reminded him of the bulldog in *Tom and Jerry*. When his colleagues seemed not to know what he was talking about, he explained: "The one who says 'Dat's my boy!'" When that didn't cheer them, he added: "Those whom VI wishes to destroy, first she demoralises".

On the drive home to Taunton, Mick Tettenborn, the West

Country rep, mulled this maxim and eventually rejected it in favour of his own long-held view that the company was not so much malign as incompetent. But he couldn't stifle the notion that after more than a decade in thrall he would think that, wouldn't he? He disliked Cy less than Runnacles, not that that was saying much, but wondered if this judgment was more occupational survival factor than evidentially based conclusion.

§

A few weeks previously George Mascaret had written a five thousand-word article on the detective novel for volume one of *The Fina A–Z of Literary Forms*. The piece – a historical outline that made perfunctory mention of the most popular and influential exponents of the genre – had to be delivered within seventy-two hours of commission, a tearing hurry that Mascaret supposed was attributable to some falling-out between the publishers and the sap they'd originally asked to do it. Having filed the work, George heard nothing more, although he had been paid, so he hesitated when someone from The Clifford Press, a mild-sounding bloke calling himself Ciaran Addey, rang to suggest a date for lunch.

Mascaret normally left his garret only to post letters and bank cheques so the offer rather threw him and he started thinking aloud.

"I could do that day but the problem is I have to be on standby in case my wife can't pick up Hector from school. If I have to be back home by then, the latest train I can get is the fourteen thirty-seven from Charing Cross. Although having said that there is the possibility of getting the fifteen-o-three from London Bridge, but it takes me longer to get there from you, so if I go for that it effectively means that I have to leave you even earlier than if I went for the fourteen thirty-seven, so there's no great advantage, although it is a possibility if there are no other options.

"I'll probably cross town by tube, but if the Central Line is still up the spout I'll have to take the bus. That's slower, too, but several routes go past you – there's the forty-eight, the one-four-nine, the two-four-three."

Ciaran Addey, who had been looking forward to a three-hour bacchanalia on exes, now said that he could see it was difficult, why didn't they make it just a quick chat over coffee? George, who had been excited by the original suggestion for the same reason, thought that this sudden change of plan was characteristic turdskinning. He spent the rest of the day re-reading the piece and convincing himself that, while it was by no objective criteria what anyone in his senses would call good, it stood favourable comparison with anything else he'd seen recently, other than perhaps the English rendition of Cervantes.

§

Jacob Pursey found management more to his taste than copywriting. He enjoyed setting sales targets, a task that generally involved dividing two-thirds of each new book's print run by the number of reps. The total number of copies produced was determined by the editors in consultation with the production department, so he could blame miscalculations on them, while he could pin any failure to sell the requisite number on the men and women in the fleet of Vauxhall Astras.

Of course it wasn't always that straightforward. Local interest was a challenge. The rep for Scotland would have to be set a higher target than the fellow in the Midlands for a book on walking the Munros. The London rep would be expected to sell more porn than VI's man in Jordan. But generally Pursey had an inexhaustible supply of people to carry the can: lashings of power and almost no responsibility.

Not that his working life was entirely sans difficulty. One of his first tasks in the new role was to intervene to save the South Asian market.

The main stockist in Pakistan was consistently extending his credit terms *ex parte*. He was currently a year late with a sum so large that it jeopardised the Far East rep's next slated tour of the region.

Pursey acted decisively, announcing the imminent publication of a biography of Mohammed Ali Jinnah, founding father of the Pakistani nation. He persuaded Ella to write a blurb and invent a highly qualified author with an imaginary chair at a real American university. Still favourably disposed to her most recent one-night stand, bastard like all men though he was, Ella arranged for this phantom work to be assigned its own International Standard Book Number, which would be taken by the trade as proof positive of its existence. Only one copy of the advanced information sheet was produced, and it was sent with a sheaf of other publicity material to Lahore. A week later VI received settlement in full and an order for the forthcoming title. Baxter Stratton wanted to close the account, but Pursey persuaded him that the customer could now be relied on to keep up to date until he received his two hundred copies, which was of course not going to be any time soon; the delay could be blamed on the inability of academics to deliver anything on schedule.

The rep's fourteen-day trip went ahead and Jacob Pursey became known as Teflon Cy.

§

George Mascaret's brain heaved on an ocean of fire as he wondered why The Clifford Press wanted to see him. By the time he arrived at their offices, he had worked himself into such a state of uncertainty that his head was throbbing. After only the most perfunctory greeting he went straight in with:

"Was my last piece okay?"

To George's surprise, Ciaran Addey had no recollection of it. He glanced in his file and said:

"Oh yes, it was perfectly fine", then went on, in an effort to create the illusion that he had thought long and hard about the content and thereby conceal the fact of the matter, which was that he had merely cut from the bottom until it fitted the grid, "I think I changed one word, but other than that I can't remember any problems at all".

Had the balance of his mind been undisturbed, George Mascaret would have judged this a result – many of his submissions to other works of the same kind were hacked around so much that he wondered why he'd been hired in the first place. One of his internal dialogues went: "Where did you get the information for your article on continental drift, George?" "From the printed version of my piece on the Defenestration of Prague, George."

But Addey's was one soft answer that didn't turn away wrath. Mascaret wouldn't give up until the quarry had been run to earth.

"Which word?"

"Oh Lord. I think it was 'nugatory'; we changed it to 'trifling'."

"Why?"

"Because we didn't think the core target readership would understand."

"How can you be sure of that?"

"Experience."

"Can they not just look it up?"

"In that case they'd need two books; and since we don't publish dictionaries that would mean we'd be encouraging money to be spent on our competitors."

"Isn't that how people build their vocabularies? I seldom read a book without a dictionary to hand, and if I don't have one beside me I make a note of the word so that I can look it up later."

In the brief ensuing silence it dawned on Mascaret that the detective novel was a red herring. The temples pulsated harder when this suspicion was confirmed.

"I'm sure that's right, but that wasn't why we wanted to talk to you."

Shit, thought Mascaret, now I've blown it: they were going to offer me a job and I've been hostile and boring. In comparable measure. Again.

But he needn't have worried.

"We're developing a series of children's books on great artists and we wondered if you might be able to help us."

The clouds dispersed.

"Great artists? Good lord, I might have the very thing." Mascaret scrabbled around in his briefcase and removed some spreads that showed Monet explaining his methods of composition to a clip-art cartoon figure of a modern child. Another of his speculative developments.

Addey looked for a moment and then said: "Do you mind if I hang onto this?"

§

The beauties of Pursey's position were several. He no longer needed to use the tube and now drove one of those cars that motoring magazines class as "executive expresses". All fuel and parking bills were paid by the company. He had gone from painstakingly dividing restaurant bills item by item between himself and his companions to painstakingly dividing restaurant bills item by item between himself and his companions, pocketing all their contributions along with the receipts and claiming the full amount back from VI, who reimbursed him without demur.

Moreover he was not following a hard act – as long as he could keep his hand out of the till he would appear in a better light than Ross Runnacles – and Baxter Stratton seldom noticed what his creations were up to. At the other end of the food chain, the reps were unfranchised: they could think what they liked and if they objected too strongly they were almost effortlessly releasable onto the job market.

As he grew in confidence, Pursey saw that his colleagues could be divided into two broad categories: those like Ella, who worked hard and didn't argue, and those like Baxter who did as little and delegated as much as possible. He came to regard VI as a chicken shack and himself as the alpha tod.

The new sales manager now embarked upon a policy that he described as empire-building and his subordinates regarded as poking his nose in where it wasn't wanted. He became particularly interventionist in the editorial department, which he surmised, largely correctly, was staffed by ineffectual lovers of literature who would do as they were told.

As he passed through the typing pool where four subs slaved over manuscripts he would walk slowly enough to glance at their work. "It should be 'Le Monde', not 'La'"; "That sentence ends with a preposition, and that is something up with which we will not put, ha ha". Often such darts hit pieces of text that the little word doctors hadn't yet come to, but none of them had the confidence to respond with anything other than "Oh, gosh, yes, thanks, Jake" or slight variations on the same submissive theme.

§

"They've seen it and they're not happy."

Jez Yaxley getting back to Mascaret with comments on the football rewrite.

"They say you've played fast and loose with the text and lost much of its meaning."

"Meaning?"

"One of the examples they cite is on page one-eight-two – have you got it there? – the bidding for the '94 World Cup."

Mascaret had the text open in front of him, but he well remembered the passage in question.

"Look, Jez, in the original, the author writes about – quote – 'an American political leader who was adopted by his stepfather, took his name and went on to the very pinnacle of the executive'. There is no mystery in this because, in context – in fact, even out of context – there is only one person it can be. So that whole dance of the seven veils in which matey implies 'there's so much more I could tell you if only the laws of libel permitted me to do so' is unpublishable for several reasons: one, because even the least knowledgeable reader will realise that it's Bill Clinton; two, because in that event Clinton or his creatures may sue your arses; and three – and this, to me, is the clincher – because it's shit. Which I remind you was your view when you gave it to me in the first place."

"I know, George, and you're quite right. Everyone here agrees that the writing was terrible and that you've done an outstanding job of salvaging it."

"Well then."

"Another thing. The opening sentence of the intro: 'I do not know where modern amateur football commenced'."

"What about it?"

"You removed it."

"Of course I did; it's rubbish."

"The author says it's rhopalic."

"Rho-what?"

"Rhopalic. A kind of sentence in which each word is one letter longer than the one before. I'd never heard of it either."

"You are having a laugh, aren't you?"

"As I say, we all know that the text was sick and that we asked you to make it well and that you cured it and we thank you for doing so. The problem is that the author's the photographer's best mate and they're saying either we stet the whole thing or they take the snaps elsewhere. So if you can just go back to the original and give it the once-over for literals, that's the best we can do in the circs."

"What about the libel?"

"I wouldn't worry. Clinton won't sue over something so petty and, in my experience, all that ever happens in such cases is that our lawyers exchange a couple of letters with theirs and we end up paying them five hundred quid. There's no more to it than that."

"What can I say? The editor's decision is final."

"Yes. But never mind. On the bright side, they say they'll never work for us again. The author also complains, by the way, that you've added a cliché to his golden prose; I'm not sure I made a note of where that came, I'd rather given up by then."

"He's just pissed off I found one he'd left out."

§

At the end of Jacob Pursey's first year at VI, the personnel department sent board members a note reminding them that the new sales manager was due a salary review. Baxter Stratton was having none of that, but marked the anniversary by taking his boy to lunch at Wheeler's.

Glancing across the restaurant, Pursey said: "I thought for a minute that was Gill Furneaux".

Stratton told him that Gill didn't eat fish, and added that, although he could see a slight resemblance, their neighbour was "not all that", whereas "Our MD is a fine-looking woman".

Pursey enthusiastically agreed: "Shame she's married".

"Yes, isn't it? Do you still see Ella?"

"Not so much now we don't work together, but we're good mates."

"Did you ever meet her twin?"

Pursey was puzzled: she hadn't even mentioned that she had one; but he wasn't going to admit not knowing something Baxter knew.

"No, not yet. But I live in hope."

"I know just what you mean. Now, what are you thinking about next year's business?"

"Strengths: I think that generally, globally, we've got a good team in place. Export is holding up well. Weaknesses: I have some reservations about Ireland, I would question whether we've got sufficient market penetration under the current arrangement."

"Do you want a change?"

"Perhaps we could give it to one of the U.K. reps, save the commission payments."

"Sounds good to me. Lose the leprechaun?"

"Sack the leprechaun."

"I leave that to you. Opportunities and threats?"

"Obviously the main chance is the new Clarissa Newnham."

"Exactly. We sold fifty thousand of the last book, and that was with Toss Testicles at the helm. I gather the next one will be her masterpiece."

"Do we know what it's about?"

"We never know anything about her books before they come in. Of course, I've not read her."

"Really?"

"No. Novels are for women and queers, but women and queers buy squillions of books. Have you met Clarrie? You must. She's something else, a real writer."

"I think the threat might lie in the editorial department. I'm not sure that some of them aren't more ivory tower than market savvy."

"Couldn't agree more. Let's shake them up, shall we? You know, the more I look at her, the more I think it's not Gill she looks like, it's that woman from Jefferson Airplane."

"Janis Joplin."

"Yes, that's the one."

After two bottles of house white they walked to the garage beneath the YMCA in Tottenham Court Road to pick up their cars. On the way Stratton expressed his view that it was very important for esprit de corps that VI people should sleep with as many of their colleagues as possible. And he said it in the grave way that people adopt when they're making autobiography sound like general principle. Putting two and two together, Pursey realised that he had just broken one of his father's golden rules.

§

"The directors have seen your concept and the unanimous view is that it's potentially the most exciting proposal we've had all year."

George Mascaret thought this could only be the softening-up that preceded bad news. He then chided himself for ingratitude: what was it with him that he always had to find the slight in praise? Then Ciaran Addey said:

"We'd like you to develop a series of six titles in this vein."

Although Mascaret knew that he wasn't about to be offered six times the fee, he suddenly got the feeling that they really wanted this to happen, and the thought was father to the hope that they might see their way to paying a bit more than usual.

But the very next line revealed that he had been right to be wary, although the blow came from an unexpected direction.

"What we're thinking is that, instead of your generic youth, the Everyboy character, each of the artists describes his techniques to his own son or daughter."

This request made George Mascaret wonder, not for the first time, if publishers just did not get it, or if they understood the commercial picture better than he ever would. Had they thought of the snag here and decided to ignore it? How could they not have? Or would he, if he had their overview, have seen that it was not a snag at all?

There are times when there is no other option than to state the obvious, which to George Mascaret in this case was:

"Not all the great artists had children. Plenty of them never did it in a way that would make procreation possible."

Ciaran Addey's face gave no clue to whether he'd thought of this before. As calm as you like he asked:

"Can you find half a dozen who did?"

George subsided into acquiescence.
"I guess that's what I do."

48

Chapter Two: Indefinite Articles

On a date that should live in infamy but won't, George Mascaret took a call from the publishing director of Skidmore, one of the firms on his mailing list. Although they'd exchanged letters over the years – suggestions one way, rejections the other – he'd never met or previously spoken to the one called Robin Peppiatt and was surprised when the voice on the phone was that of a young female.

"We've looked at *Title Deeds*, and although we think it's got legs it really doesn't quite fit in with our current publication programme. But we wish you all luck with it elsewhere."

Although nothing like quick on the uptake, after more than a quarter of a century in the business George had got the idea of it well enough to realise that if that was all she had to say she wouldn't have rung, so he threw in no more than an "Alas" in the hope that it wouldn't interrupt her flow. It didn't.

"Don't despair, we've got a better idea. I mean, an even better idea."

This was courtesy as afterthought, but it was still courtesy, and Mascaret acknowledged it with something between a snort and a chuckle.

"We're aware of some of your other work and what we'd like you to do is develop..." – a brief pause and a kind of line crackle that may have masked prompting offstage – "No, that's not right – we'd like you to write, yes write, a book of forty thousand words entitled…" – another moment of dead air as Robin moved from babbling to reading – "*101 Reasons for Staying Single*. We can give you plenty of time and the money isn't bad, either, but we can't pay you a royalty, I'm afraid, it'd have to be a fee, half up front, the rest on publication."

§

Jacob Pursey added Clarissa Newnham to the circle of his acquaintance at one of those after-hours bookshop events where the reading classes get to ask authors about their working methods and their output. The questions are generally of two types: deferential-to-fawning and impenetrably obscure. Knowing the form, Pursey arrived late after killing time window-shopping outside Jermyn Street tailors. He clocked his star author leant against a philosophy section with a drink in her hand doing convo with some other cadaverous broad, whom Clarissa introduced as Solveig Rawtenstall. Pursey knew the name, which was big on the Hutchinson fiction list. They looked like they were talking to each other in order to discourage approaches from the punters.

As they chatted, Pursey noticed that the other two were struggling to keep straight faces. Figuring their glasses contained more than orange juice, he blanked it at first, but eventually he was moved to ask them what was funny. Solveig apologised for their rudeness; Clarissa explained:

"We were looking through that" – she pointed to a nearby display table bearing piles of *Croak Monsieur*, a comedy thriller by a celebrity chef-journalist.

"What about it?"

"It's hard to know where to start; such a bad writer; so slack."

"Incontinent," added Solveig slurrily.

"Not so much hard-boiled as half-hatched."

Another shared snigger.

Pursey opened the work in question: "Go on, show me a bit."

The women glanced at each other. Then Clarissa touched Pursey's wrist and told him: "It's impossible to explain. You have to be a writer to understand these things."

§

The Lord giveth and the Lord taketh away, George Mascaret reminded himself when hard upon the good news from Robin at Skidmore came trouble with the painting series. After skimming a couple of biographies – "A shilling life will give you all the facts" – Mascaret gave The Clifford Press a name to approve as the first case for treatment. They mulled his suggestion for a week, by the end of which their own research revealed that this Rembrandt van Rijn he'd identified had been heterosexual to a fault and had loads of children, many of them in wedlock. Confident that their core market would find nothing to disapprove, they gave Mascaret what they called the green light.

Thus encouraged, Mascaret chose for discussion *Aristotle with the Bust of Homer*. He wrote, sketched and laid out in rough the detailed first draft of a twenty-four-page book in which the artist demonstrated his methods of composition to his son Titus, who at the time of the painting's execution would have been ten or eleven years of age.

The publishers liked the Mascaret treatment when they first saw it, but the longer they looked at it the more they worried that Middle American seventh-graders would never have heard of Aristotle and be unaware that the Homer in question was the putative author of the *Iliad* rather than one of the principal characters in an animated cartoon series. Mascaret's offer to gloss them was rejected on the grounds that that would make the work too fusty and academic. Ciaran Addey suggested instead one of the artist's last self-portraits, three works of 1669. This began as no more than a random thought, an attempt to sound positive while creating the as it happened false impression that he knew a bit about the subject. However, his attitude changed after Mascaret pointed out that Rembrandt could not have discussed these works with Titus or any of his other children, because by that year they had all predeceased him. Addey and his masters then decided that these paintings were the sine qua non; without them the whole deal was off.

§

The Newnham debacle wasn't the first time Jacob Pursey had had the feeling that people – especially those he'd met since his promotion – viewed him as untutored and coarse. The reason for their misjudgment seemed clear: everyone expected a sales manager to be a wide boy in a tick-tack man's suit with repartee along the lines of "If you take a hundred copies of that, darling, I might be able to do you a special favour later". They saw the office, not the holder. Only a fool would have sought to dispel such notions by inveighing against them: acknowledgement was half an admission. He determined to show them from now on that he was more *uomo universale* than colporteur.

A few days later, as Pursey on a promenade through the editorial department was demanding that the "who" in "a man who she thought was ill" be changed to "whom", he noticed a bloke off the telly leaving Willy Lechler's office.

This Willy, editorial supremo, was sometimes described by colleagues as a card, but Pursey quickly dismissed the intended allusion to the joker; the value of this little billiard ball of a manikin could never possibly have been higher than that of the two of clubs.

"Was that James Cree? What did he want?"

"To see his book in print."

"Is he going to?"

"I wouldn't have thought so. He's been touting it ever since he announced he'd be standing down at the next election. There's not a commissioning editor in London who hasn't seen it and not a one of us who would touch it with a disinfected bargepole."

"His name will sell."

"It may be that you can get it into bookshops…"

"No maybe about it."

"Indeed. But we'll never get newspaper serialisation and an earthquake won't shift it off the shelves. No gossip, no scandal, no revelations, just procedural stuff about the mechanism for removing a party leader. And of course screeds and screeds of vanity and self-regard."

"Can I read it?"

"Of course."

Willie slapped the top page of the biggest manuscript on his desk, a thousand typed pages, a quarter of a million words. Then Pursey said:

"On second thoughts, why don't you and I have lunch?"

§

The collapse of the Rembrandt left Mascaret free to devote more time to *101 Reasons*. After spending the greater part of the day doodling and almost completing the *Times'* crossword, he decided that the only way he was going to compose a contents list was by returning to the bosom of his family. He rose from his desk and went downstairs, where Hector,

Charley and Agnes (named after his *mémé* and pronounced the French way, though written perversely without the grave) were watching children's television.

When he joined them in the sitting room he received neither acknowledgement nor flicker of recognition. As usual. This was on the point of annoying him but then he decided that if they hadn't seen him as part of their lives they would have got up and greeted him courteously as they had been trained to do with visitors. In the light of this conclusion he consoled himself with the thought that the ruder they are, the stronger the bond.

After sitting for a few minutes to one side of their line of vision, he ventured a wave and a *"Salut, mes enfants"*.

"What are you doing here?" asked Agnes, without taking her eyes off the screen.

"Just a pastoral visit."

No response.

"Do you know what a pastoral visit is?"

"No," said Charley, "but I fear we're about to find out".

"Why can't you ever just tell us anything?" sighed Hector.

"A pastoral visit is when a religious leader, like the Pope…"

The children opened their mouths wide and tapped their palms over them.

"You may affect ennui now, O generation of vipers, but one day you'll look back on moments like these and, quoting Elton John, say 'I should have listened to my old man'."

"Really?"

"Yes, really. And do you know which of Elton John's songs that comes from?"

"Was that a quiz question?"

"Yes."

"Dunno then."

"Is that your final answer?"

"Yes, Papa, it is. We've had a lovely day; we'll take the money. Thank you."

"'Goodbye Yellow Brick Road.' That's b-r-i-c-k, before you say anything."

Having made his presence felt and outstayed his welcome in a single masterful stroke, George wandered complacently into the kitchen where Vivienne, just back from work, was making dinner. Like an official at passport control, she asked him the reason for his visit; he told her about the book.

"I can see it might be hard to restrict it to so few."

"I'm pleased you say that," said George, "because I can't think of any…"

"I hope you're not going to ask me to write it for you."

"… apart, I was going to add, from these I've jotted down."

He often did this to her when he was stuck. He found it had a laxative effect on his costive prose; she, although she never said so, thought it reminiscent of a child showing off its potty to a Freudian parent. George unfolded a scrap of paper and read aloud:

"Reasons for not getting married the first: you won't get dobbed in it on the phone when you don't want to answer it."

"You'll have to spell it out more clearly than that."

"Well, you know, if you live alone and you're avoiding someone, you just don't pick up, do you?"

"Speak for yourself. Some of us welcome human contact."

"How often have I said, 'Tell them I'm not in' and the next thing I hear is one of you saying, 'I'll just get him for you'? And I've got four hundred words per entry."

"Ah, right," said Vivienne, face momentarily enveloped in steam as she drained the cauliflower.

"Two: you don't have to ask for things that have gone missing."

Vivienne said: "Before you and the children, I knew that whenever I went to the bathroom the radio would be on the station I'd left it on".

George made a note, then added:

"You can open every letter that comes to the house, without having to check the name on the envelope".

As Vivienne was dishing up, she thought of another: "You don't have to clean the bath after every use. Not that anyone bothers except me".

Hector objected that he always cleaned it. His sisters told him there was no evidence that he even knew where the bathroom was.

After dinner the children dispersed to their rooms.

"I saw this today, thought you might be interested."

Vivienne handed George a Hatchards bag containing a book of football supporters' songs.

"You could make the same sort of thing into a series, say a twenty-four-page book on each club."

"Not a bad idea." George checked the spine. "Oh look, it's by the same people, Skidmore. I could put in some chants as well. A child's introduction to the club he's going to support."

"Or she."

"Yes, dear. Like West Ham fans don't usually talk about the Hammers, that's what outsiders call them; they call them the Irons."

"If you say so, dear. When's this *101 Reasons* thing for?"

"The end of the month."

"So why are you here? You should be typing. Go on, bugger off back where you belong."

§

Jacob Pursey and Baxter Stratton timetabled weekly catch-up meetings that usually took place twice a month because they both knew that punctual and regular attendance at anything sends the wrong message, suggests someone with time on his hands.

At their next get-together they agreed that, home and abroad, performance overall was as good as they could be expected to expect it to be. Their searchlights raked the sales-by-area printouts and found nothing untoward; they told each other that everything was hunky-dory. Everything, that is, apart from what Baxter called "the spanner in the woodpile": a lower turnover increase in Iberia than in any other part of Europe. Having either failed to notice or chosen to ignore that Spanish and Portuguese were the only major languages of the continent that did not yet have dedicated volumes in the VI Philologia series, they decided that the answer to the problem should be sought on an executive field trip. Normally such an expedition would be undertaken by the sales manager alone but, since the local agent was based in Barcelona, Stratton decided that he and Pursey needed to go there together.

"By the way, how d'you do with Clarrie?"

"Brilliant. Instant rapport."

"She's a honey. I knew you'd get on."

§

It was more than a week since George Mascaret had read Hector a bedtime story, and meanwhile the boy wondered who the man of the island might be. As they settled down together, the father with the Dent Everyman edition, the son following in a version produced by Clowes and Sons of London and Beccles, it emerged that the feral creature was none other than cheese-loving Ben Gunn. A couple of pages further on, Hector interrupted his father with:

"You missed out a word."

George was about to say that he venerated this author's work as holy writ and he would no more omit a syllable of it than break wind in a cathedral when he saw that in Hector's version it indeed said "And with that he winked and pinched me hard", whereas in his own there was no opening conjunction.

If this was how publishers treated text, how was anyone to know what Stevenson actually wrote, even scholars, apart from the very few who had read the manuscript, if it were extant? Neither edition gave any clue that there was more than one version of the original; each purported to be complete and unabridged. For a moment the question of whether the author had or had not used the word became a matter of obsessional importance to Mascaret. If it wasn't an echt RLS "and", it was an "and" that had been interpolated by some lily-gilding desk editor turd. Alternatively, if it was in the original, it confirmed that nice customs – notwithstanding that in Mascaret's view the avoidance of starting sentences with this part of speech was neither nice nor necessary – curtsy to great kings.

Mascaret recalled two cognate events that still riled him. Once he'd written to *The Daily Telegraph* to point out that its lead reviewer had misquoted a line from George Meredith's *Modern Love* – "We are deceived by what is false within" rather than "We are betrayed by what is false within". The literary editor made light of this, replying that it was "an error in one word only".

The other was an altercation with a colleague who'd added an "of" to Ben Jonson's verdict on Shakespeare: "I loved the man on this side idolatry".

"If you don't believe I've got it right," Mascaret had begun, determined to hold out for accuracy, "look it up". But even as he spoke he felt the fluids of his resistance trickling away into the sand. "Check the *Oxford Dictionary of Quo…*bollocks, whatever." These were lasting reminders of the impossibility of getting what you have written published.

After Hector and his siblings were asleep and Vivienne was on the phone to her mother (at least an hour of anyone's time), Mascaret gathered from another of his shilling lives that the original publisher of *Treasure Island* had lost the drawing by Lloyd Osbourne that inspired the novel. Bloody typical.

That night George Mascaret had his anxiety dream, in which a publisher tells him that the "new" in "New York" should be lower case because, while "York" is a proper noun, "new" is just a qualifying epithet. Mascaret cries "You know-nothing fuckpig" and wakes up pouring sweat generated by fear that he will never work again.

§

To celebrate completion of her eighth novel, *Behind A Dream*, Clarissa Newnham is taken to lunch at The Ivy by her agent, Vernon Kanzell, an enthusiast in a bow tie.

"So have you actually handed it in yet?"

"I'm seeing Max Volkmer next week."

Kanzell discerned here a window of opportunity; although several times previously he'd had it slammed shut on his fingers, he nevertheless tried again to climb in:

"Before you part with it, Clarrie, remember that

Transsworld will give you more than ten times what you're presently being paid as an advance."

"Vernon, I've told you, I owe everything to VI. When I went there I was a resting actress, grateful for a bit of light filing. Then when I showed Max my first novel he really believed in it and got behind it; the rest you know."

"In Andrey Sinyavsky there's a hundred-word fable about a poor man who meets three people in a forest. He's afraid they may be thieves, and tells them as much, but they say 'We're not going to hurt you; let's just talk; if you're nervous, you can stand a few paces away'. Then one of them asks him: 'You wouldn't have a piece of bread? We haven't eaten for three days.' So he gives them all the food he has. The story ends: 'Later they were caught and shot in town'."

"I don't get it; I'd need to see it on the page."

"The point is, not all thieves say stand and deliver. The smart ones make sure you don't even know you're being robbed."

"I'm not blind to Max's faults, Vernon, but he's an important part of my life."

"So are your milk teeth, but aren't you glad you're shot of them?"

For a while they spoke of other things. But Kanzell hadn't succeeded by allowing his clients to dictate the discussion agenda. Half a bottle later he asked her:

"When did VI last pay you a royalty?"

"Royalty? On the hardback?"

"Why, yes. Under the terms of your previous agreements, they pay you for your hardbacks in three stages…"

"One on signature, one on delivery, one on publication."

"There you are: what can I tell you you don't know already? Then what?"

"Then what I get a fee from VI when they sell the paperback rights and thereafter I get royalties from the paperback publisher."

"Yes, but what about continuing sales of the hardback? You get nothing more than the advance?"

"I'd have to check my accounts, but not that I can think of, no."

"And the advance is the same as it always was, a thousand pounds?"

"If I was any good at this I'd be running a shop."

"If you were even better at this you'd be letting me do the whole thing, getting what they call 'the full service', rather than ringfencing one of your most golden geese out of sentimental attachment to a publisher who would, frankly, sell his mother's jewel through a hole in a fence."

"Vernon, really. Have you chosen your main course? I fancy the turbot."

§

To chart the progress of *101 Reasons*, George Mascaret drew the outline of a long thin tube with a big circle at the bottom which he coloured in in red. He then calibrated the stem of this thermometer-like artwork with twenty-eight horizontal bars, each of which represented his daily quota of fifteen hundred words or three and a half entries. Still eighty-eight short of his headword target after a week, one quarter of the time available, he had coloured in only four sections, but he had drawn so many bass clefs and treble clefs and funny faces around the edges that it was no longer easy to see that the blank sheet with which he started had originally been white. There was nothing for it but to draw a new thermometer, this time with only twenty bars, each now representing two thousand words a day. Still his time had not been entirely wasted: he'd reached the end of Chapter Five of *Don Quixote*, "In which the story of our knight's misfortune is continued", although he remembered so little of what had gone before that he knew he'd have to start again.

Not all his activities were displacement. Other paid work demanded some of his time. The Denver publishers queried a reference in *The Modern Arab World*, another of their forthcoming titles, to a network of pipes and irrigation channels that brings water from an artesian basin under the Libyan Sahara to the coastal lowlands. Concerned that the name of the waterway, The Great Man-Made River, was politically incorrect, they asked Mascaret why he hadn't flagged it and told him to change it to "The Great Artificial River".

Resentful that this was diverting him from his greater or at least more pressing purpose, Mascaret drafted a reply that began "You asked me to act in an oversight capacity and I took you at your word". He then scribbled another that dealt with the matter as po-facedly as they had approached it and warned them that to change an official name for such a feeble reason might result in their being held up to public ridicule.

Not long afterwards he concluded that he should just keep quiet and do what they asked. Which raised again the great imponderable that hung over all his dealings with Americans: why did they employ foreign dogs to do this work? Surely there were literate and educated people in the United States who would be more accessible to them and perhaps even cheaper than he was? Maybe he failed to see himself as others saw him, a stylist and the cause of style in others. But if that was reality rather than phantasmagoria, why did the world (especially its western hemisphere) habitually ignore or contradict him? He knew nothing of economics, but he did wonder how much Anglo-U.S. trade was as pointless as this.

§

At a wine bar on Fleet Street, Jacob Pursey, who thought his companion would make better use of his time starving in a garret while producing one haiku a year, and Willie Lechler, who regarded the creature sitting opposite him as something that Jonathan Swift, had he been living at that hour, might have rejected as his model for the Yahoo because it was just too parodically uncouth, demonstrated one of the codifiable certainties of commercial life: that the greater two business colleagues' mutual contempt, the higher the level of bonhomie they display to each other. Unless they can keep a safe distance, which for these two was not an option: they were like a White Star liner and the ocean floor.

As Pursey turned the first wine bottle upside down before the antipasti had even been ordered, Lechler asked:

"Are we going to pay for this ourselves?"

"Hell, no, I'll put it through as market research."

"My dear chap, I can't allow that; it should come out of my budget."

"Do you have any spare?"

"Not masses, but I run a tight ship."

"How many editors have you got?"

"Four in-house; the ones you sometimes talk to."

"Eenie, Meenie, Minie and Homo."

Lechler had heard this appellation before and indeed sometimes used it himself, but he was damned if he was going to conspire with this dreadful pushy oik. He smiled to show that he wasn't amused and said:

"Tim, Tom, Colin and Rufus. They're very good at what they do."

"The best in London, there can be no doubt, but I was just wondering, from a commercial viewpoint, about volume throughput. I mean, we currently publish two hundred new titles a year, so they each do about a book a week. That's not a lot, is it?"

"They also handle reprints and new editions."

"But if we could produce fifty per cent more books without taking on any more staff…"

"That won't happen."

"Why so sure?"

"Because if you increase their workload they'll vote with their feet."

"Not easy in this climate: look at the price of oil, the stock market, the flaky pound. What if I could pick up a few nouveautés here and there, based on, for example, what W.H. Smith want?"

Thinking that this barbarian would enter the Eternal City of English letters over his dead body, Lechler tried to look encouraging; he replied:

"I'd certainly put anything that came to us that way in front of the editorial committee".

Thinking I bet you would, you time-serving scumsucker, Pursey thanked him before continuing:

"What about sponsored books?"

"Of course we do many – that history of Rio Negro Mining was financed by the company."

"And what about books paid for by individuals?"

Vanity publishing? Surely salesmen were bred to loathe such enterprise because it brought them the worst of all worlds: meddling authors who spent their extensive leisure looking for their books in shops that had refused to stock them for the perfectly sound reason that they were of no interest to anyone half normal. Lechler had no idea what this shit was up to, but he knew that it was no good.

§

Halfway through his allotted time, George Mascaret was now making significant progress. He'd almost completed the list of topics, among the highlights of which was: "You don't have to account for your movements. If you want to stop off in Bath on your way from London to Penzance, you won't have to demonstrate that it was to admire the architecture rather than for some assignation".

As he hacked away, unconnected, irrelevant ideas occurred to him and he broke off to scribble them down. Having been transferred from brain to paper, some of these were unintelligible; others he was confident would be of interest to readers in the unlikely event that he could find a suitable case in which to display them and then get a publisher involved. Regardless of the quality of his tangential thoughts, however, they were all distractions from the job in hand.

One typical day he spent an hour on a single entry for *101 Reasons* and then twice as long musing about the pointlessness of lit-crit. If a work is poor, it needs improving; if it's good, it requires no explanation. Most of the critical writings on, for example, *Paradise Lost* are concerned with the complexity of the knots in which Milton tied himself while trying to depict God – omniscient, omnipotent and definitively good but who permitted human suffering – and the fallen angels, who were evil but artistically inspiring.

He wrote in his Journal: "If the U.S.P. of Christianity is 'Whosoever believeth in me (i.e., J.C.) shall not perish but have everlasting life', why do even the most faithful have doubts about a God who permits His creations to wage war and writhe in pain? Has none of them ever thought that, compared to an eternity of harp-playing on a cloud, a few years of earthly agony are no more than a fleabite?"

His mind then wandered onto popular verse, works that give poetry a good name. Take "Dying Speech of an Old Philosopher", the one that begins "I strove with none for none was worth my strife". It's in almost every anthology, so people must think it's good. But what exegesis does it require other than that it's a quatrain rhymed ABAB and it says what it says? Hence the dearth of studies of Walter Savage Landor; hence too the author's absence from syllabuses and reading lists. It seemed that the critical attention paid to an author was almost directly proportional to his failure as an artist – if the writer got it right he transcended criticism and was therefore seldom discussed. There are more studies of Virgil than of Martial; theses on tin-eared, doom-laden Thomas Hardy are greatly more numerous than those on peerless P.G. Wodehouse. In the case of Shakespeare, the opposite applies: even though he's the best, he still has innumerable critics, most of whom feel they have to speculate about what he was trying to say: the milk of human kindness or the milk of humankindness? But this is mere impertinence: the beauty is that he could mean either or both – "Take him for all in all" and all that.

§

As Jacob Pursey approached VI's offices at a civilised hour one morning he saw on the pavement outside a knot of colleagues gathered around a recently drawn-up Bentley. One of them opened the door and they all inclined their heads respectfully as an old man with a grey moustache slowly alighted from the back seat and shuffled with the aid of a walking stick towards the main entrance. By the time they reached the lift, Pursey had barged his way into the heart of the action and insinuated himself next to the great man. As the doors closed the flunkeys and toadies maintained a reverential silence but Pursey was cut from a different cloth.

"Good morning, sir. Jake Pursey, sales manager."

Max Volkmer offered a limp handshake but said nothing.

Noticing under the chairman's arm the manuscript of *Behind A Dream*, Pursey asked:

"Read any great books lately?"

Max Volkmer looked for a moment as if he was not going to dignify this with a response but then said:

"I've just re-read *War and Peace* on a cruise, but it was in a most unsatisfactory French translation so I threw it overboard off Cape St Vincent."

Pursey thought this was brilliant, but the others in the lift and the numerous colleagues and friends to whom he subsequently quoted it as an exemplary insight into the workings of an outstanding intellect were unanimous in the view that the chairman had been taking the piss.

On reaching the executive floor, Volkmer and his attendants took so long to get out that the doors closed before Pursey could follow them and he had to walk back down to his office from the top level.

§

At the eleventh hour Mascaret fulfilled his commitment to submit a complete list of one hundred and one topics to Skidmore for approval. If they'd objected to any of them he'd have been in dead lumber but he knew that, given the tightness of the schedule, they were unlikely to do so. Robin Peppiatt was either naive or canny enough to restrict her comments to:

"This looks super, George; you've more or less done it already. Thank you so much; we're all really excited and look forward to receiving the finished manuscript next week."

George knew she meant well, but he found her nonspecific enthusiasm dispiriting. By the time she mentioned that she'd sent a cheque for the first instalment the previous day, he was so downcast that he could scarcely bring himself to sound grateful. The mood stayed on him and he did no more work until the arrival of the post revealed that she was as good as her gushing word.

§

"Stratton, we have a problem."

Gill Furneaux recounted her meeting with the chairman. Max Volkmer, she said, hadn't raised his voice or threatened her; he hadn't even used hyperbole; he had spoken in the measured tones of an octogenarian who was accustomed to getting his own way; indeed, there was nothing in his demeanour to suggest that he even knew what dissent was. Insofar as he was the employer telling his chief executive how it was and should be, this was not unexpected; what surprised Gill was the menace that he introduced into a rational statement of the facts in the case. Even his pose – resting his hands on the crook of his upright stick – was somehow more intimidating than muggers with knuckledusters.

"I had a most pleasant lunch yesterday with Clarissa Newnham. I hadn't seen her in more than a year. A lovely woman. She gave me this…", he inclined his gaze towards the manuscript on his knees. "I read it last night. That it will not win any of the prestigious awards for fiction is more a reflection of the judges' petty internecine rivalries than of the work itself, which in my view surpasses even her own previous achievements. However, my critical response is immaterial; my commercial instinct tells me that you will make it outsell Catherine Cookson."

Just as Gill was starting to think that the old man had come a long way from his country seat merely to do a Henry V before Harfleur he came to the sharp point.

"Also during our most pleasant lunch, Clarissa alerted me to what I imagine can only be an unfortunate but chronic accounting error. It appears that we owe her rather a large sum of money. Embarrassingly, she hinted that her remaining with this company is now dependent upon our righting the matter without delay."

Having joined VI only three years previously, Gill knew nothing of this state of affairs and how it had developed. Max told her:

"Clarissa Newnham is a lady. Although I would never presume to describe myself as a gentleman, it is in the image of one that I constantly strive to appear. Thus inhibited, we regard discussions of pelf as too vulgar for our refined sensibilities. In the circumstances, some might say that over the years I have derived greater benefit from this reticence than she has, but that must be a matter for them. Now, finally, the music seems to have stopped and it is time for us to render unto Caesar's wife that which is hers. Naturally she does not know the exact amount in question and neither do I. Nevertheless, I am sure you will agree that this situation cannot be allowed to continue."

Gill made appropriate "What in our house?" noises and promised to pay Clarissa Newnham fully up to date instanter.

And having made that undertaking she was shortly afterwards horrified to discover that the sum in question was equivalent to VI's annual turnover in Australasia.

"So what we gonna do, Bax?"

"The main thing is not to panic. Leave it with me."

Gill almost remarked on the contradiction inherent in this answer but as Stratton was her only ally she managed to keep the thought to herself. When he left her alone, she drafted a grovelling letter to Clarissa Newnham but then thought better of leaving her dabs at the crime scene so she wrote a cheque for a six-figure sum, got the accountant to sign it, stuck it in an envelope with a compliments slip, ordered her secretary to write the address and find a stamp, then slipped out of the office, past the post room, and dropped it into a pillar box herself.

§

On the eve of the deadline, George Mascaret read through the completed manuscript of *101 Reasons for Staying Single*, typed an invoice for the second payment, scribbled a covering note, stuffed all the material into a jiffy bag and took it by train to the offices of Skidmore, where he handed it in at reception ten minutes before the official closing time and an hour after all right-thinking staff, including Robin Peppiatt, had gone home. His children scorned him for undertaking this journey – what, they reasonably asked, was wrong with the Royal Mail? – but Mascaret warned them of the dangers of giving hostages to fortune. They yawned and waved him off before he could give them his other reason, which was that like late-night Doctor Faustus he just wanted to get away from his books.

§

"I've talked to Teflon Cy and he's confident we've got it covered. We're presently sitting on a fifty-grand order from a new account in Wales, which will now be despatched tomorrow, and he's been on to James Cree, M.P., who's said he'll pay for all the printing and marketing of his memoirs at a price that'll give us a six-times mark-up on the actual cost."

When Stratton told her how much that was worth, Gill pulled a face and said:

"Not enough."

"That's not all. Next week we're going to give the Spanish agent an exclusive. Under the terms he'll have to kick out the competition and give all his warehouse space to VI product. It'll cost him a hundred kay to reach the requisite stock level."

Quickly and not necessarily accurately calculating that this sale would yield only a tenth of that amount in profit, Gill asked him:

"What else?"

"We've binned that seditious prick Mahoney and given Ireland to the London rep, a saving of twenty grand a year."

Gill thought all that sounded like the germ of a way to go, but she wasn't going to say so. Still Stratton detected a lightening of her mood.

"So if you're happy with that, perhaps we should…?"

He misread her.

"I'm looking to save my arse, not waggle it in your face."

"Consider it saved; not that it was ever in danger."

"You say that. Max Volkmer may look like an old sweetie but he'd have the lungs out of your ribcage like a shot if he thought it was expedient to do so."

"Look, Gill, this is no sweat. Forget any shit about 'Never trust a man who says, "trust me"'; when I tell you we've got it covered, we've got it covered, all right?"

Again no reply, which Stratton took as encouraging.

"What about tonight?"

"No, no. Out of the question." She waved her hand as if wafting away a bad smell.

Stratton rose to leave. As he opened the door to the outer office, Gill added:

"You've just explained something I've often wondered about."

He raised his eyebrows expectantly.

"Your nickname."

"I didn't know I had one."

"Well you do. You are known to the other ranks as...", she pointed to the door and Stratton let it close again in the interests of security.

"The Toothy Rapist."

Stratton started to grin but thinking that in the circumstances doing so might make him look a berk he covered his mouth with his hand and made off alone to the pub.

§

"Now it is too late for action, too soon for contrition", George Mascaret reflected as he waited for Skidmore's response. Reading his submission again and again he sometimes thought "What genius I had when I wrote that" but more frequently noticed literals and infelicities of style. Which were regrettable but not irremediable – Robin would find some of them (and no doubt, if she was like every other editor with whom he'd ever worked, insert a few of her own device) but he could put them all right at proof stage. He then wondered – not for the first time – why he so often thought in sayings and quotations, even those of people like Eliot whom he couldn't stand. Perhaps they were crutches for a mind that, though active, was lacking in originality. But he consoled himself with the thought that the creative process was not straightforward. Sometimes rhymes and mots he had learned many years previously came back to him in altered form. Often this was simple inversion – "Any storm in a port", his stock comment on extramarital liaisons. Not infrequently they were gibberish, like the misheard lyrics of pop songs. But occasionally, very occasionally, the material coalesced into a new form that, while not aboriginal – nothing is – rendered its antecedents unidentifiable. Thus while his readers (if he had any, which he doubted) might think his work was crap, they could never trace its origins and inspiration, in the way that, for example, the writings of Evelyn Waugh revealed a debt to Ronald Firbank.

George Mascaret thus concluded that imagination is decaying memory, an aperçu that he wrote up at length in his Journal.

§

Most publication dates are no big deal. Not a firework is lit; the author doesn't get a telegram of congratulations or a bunch of flowers. They aren't even really dates: books just seep out of the warehouse and into the shops up to a month before and as long as a month after their promulgated time. This is often annoying for booksellers and had always disappointed Clarissa Newnham, so after the sales of her third novel demonstrated her durability, VI took to throwing a party to give each of her new books a bit of a send-off.

That for *Behind A Dream* was held at Kettner's, chosen for its proximity to the Groucho Club, the preferred venue, which, by the time VI got round to making the booking, was full on the required night. In attendance were several of the author's literary mates, whose number included Kingsley Amis, Anthony Burgess, Jon Silkin; a bunch of journos; hangers-on who turned up at all such do's – Max Volkmer said he wished he had the balls to greet them with "How lovely to see you; if I'd known you were coming I'd have invited you" – and all those who had been involved or who claimed involvement in the transformation of the manuscript into what they described as a blockbuster.

Just as people go to dinner parties with gifts for their hosts –

flowers, chocolates, a bottle of wine – it seemed as if everyone entered the function room with a special word or a set phrase that was going to get used during the course of the evening. Noticing Jacob Pursey moving through the crowd like an assassin, Willie Lechler told him that he was a cork. At least that was how it sounded. Although bemused, Pursey didn't admit not knowing what it meant because that would have been a sign of weakness. Since Willie sounded like he was from out of town, Pursey decided it was some regional term of approbation – ebullient, buoyant, irrepressible, that kind of thing – and was quite chuffed by the description: it rang true and symbolised the obeisance of the pack animal to the dominant male.

Vernon Kanzell, in a white suit, worked the room, telling all the famous authors that the hay in his stable was lusher than that in their present agents' and pressing them to come and talk to him about it over lunch. He was even nice to some of the publishers. Not the management, whom he regarded with a disdain that was entirely reciprocal. Baxter Stratton had once in his cups told Clarissa that everyone at VI found Kanzell too mad to deal with. Clarissa shrewdly concluded from this that Vernon must be doing a good job and the remark thus helped ensure that author and agent would be together forever. But Kanzell was charming to the junior editors, giving them carefully crafted apocryphal revelations about his authors – an England footballer who refused a ghost for his autobiography; a philosopher who, having been commissioned to write a life of

Bertrand Russell, delivered a manuscript that was two-thirds biography and one-third love letter to his own wife, a penance for having been caught in flag del with his research assistant while the book was on the stocks. If the workers alluded to their own creative aspirations – they nearly all had novels in their bottom drawers – Kanzell encouraged them to send him the manuscripts, although he covered himself by saying that he didn't do a lot of fiction. His main theme was the merits of "vertical publishers" – those who produce both hardback and paperback editions of every book on their lists. Most houses now did that as a matter of course; he chose this as his leitmotif for the evening to remind everyone that VI only did Clarissa's hardbacks.

Baxter Stratton told those he spoke to of his excitement at being involved in a communications industry that brought both pleasure and enlightenment to the masses. *Fructating,* he called it. He complimented his female colleagues on their party frocks in a way that he thought was suave. Ella told him she bet he said that to all the girls. "Of course," Baxter agreed, "but in your case I really mean it. If I was ten years younger…"

"Aah," said Ella, "but what if I were ten years older?"

Stratton couldn't think of a reply; his default smile was less lascivious than usual and he put his hand over his mouth as it opened.

Max Volkmer made a short speech in which he called *Behind A Dream* "a landmark publication" and said that although VI was known by some as "the world's last remaining horizontal publisher" it was a firm whose firmness was based on a simple and foolproof marketing plan: "Produce a bloody good-looking book and sell the hell out of it". The microphone brought out his accent, which though strong in his nonage was now seldom discernible and had thus rendered obsolete the name by which he had originally been known among his senior staff, Mittel Max, Mittel as in European.

Clarissa came to the microphone and replied: "As I lie in my hammock I know that it is held up by two staunch Poles – Vernon over there and Max. There may sometimes be tension between them, but it is that which makes taut the framework and comfortable my repose". She then thanked everyone for coming and expressed the hope that the book would sell "thousands and thousands and thousands of copies".

As the applause died down, Gill Furneaux, who had stood throughout alone in a corner of the room, caught Baxter's eye and motioned with her head towards the door.

Jacob Pursey, well oiled, found himself with the four editors who had come to dread his footfall behind their desks. The one known as Eenie asked Pursey about Cath, not because he wanted his opinion but partly because he was just trying to hold his end up conversationally and partly (although he didn't mention this) because he had that very lunchtime snuck off for an interview at her father's firm.

"*De mortuis nisi bene,*" said Pursey authoritatively.

"Isn't it '*de mortuis nil nisi bonum*'?" said the one known as Meenie as lightly as he could.

"Pedant," said Pursey.

"A pedant is anyone whose standards of accuracy are slightly higher than your own", said the one known as Minie. The one known as Homo later described that remark as "the loyal suicide note".

§

In the quiet time after the parturition of the book, Mascaret drove into the Sussex countryside and went for a walk, away from his books, away from his typewriter, away from his family, and took stock of himself. Not, he knew, a big job, but the work expanded to fill the couple of hours available. The thing about writing, he decided as he reached the Channel coast, was that if you do it, you get on and do it. But then, as he headed back to the car, he thought woe betide you if you pause to reflect on how you gain your effects, such as they may be, because as soon as you do you stop being able to achieve them. Why didn't he write something worthwhile? An epic poem; a bildungsroman, an apologia, something that would show people he'd never met, and perhaps some as yet unborn, what he was like as a person and that he had some abilities other than the capacity to extrapolate intended meanings from rubbishy scrawlings. Of course, his children would speak to posterity by their very being, even if they never mentioned him, but they did not know his whole story, and some of the details – if not the essential truth – would get lost in their retelling. But then again, how much of his life was interesting? Many autobiographers placed themselves among "those who were truly great" (the vom-inducing phrase was Stephen Spender's), but were their assumptions always justified? Another reason he didn't write what he called a proper book was that no one would pay him up front to do so. And for as long as people kept giving him commissions he had no time or leftover energy to do anything else. But that was just an excuse and he knew it. He had always enjoyed writing – or, at least, to put it in Stevenson's more precise terms, he enjoyed having written – but he was now doing it only for the money and wouldn't unsheathe his ballpoint for any other reason. And was there not a name for people who do pleasurable things only for money?

§

"This was the greatest city on earth to me once", said Baxter Stratton to Jacob Pursey as they sat in a café on Balmes. "When I first came here, Franco was in charge. I wasn't a fan, mind you, but he kept order, made sure the peasants and the commies knew their place. What is more, he banned Catalan nationalism. At the time that seemed to me like a bad thing, but now, looking at it, I don't know so much.

"This street", he pointed to Gran Via on their map, "used to be called Avenida José Antonio in honour of Primo de Rivera, founder of the Falange. This", he pointed at Diagonal, "was

Avenida Generalissimo, named after the great leader himself. All you had to do to establish a rapport with the Cats was to call these roads by what are now their official names. So easy, just like that. All the advantages of being a co-conspirator with none of the dangers of being worked over by the Guardia Civil, who didn't even bother to arrest you and duff you up in private; more than once I saw them take a firm hand with pissed foreigners in full view of the world. Batons and all, nothing serious but highly unattractive to those raised in effete liberal democracies like ours. Then Franco died and instead of the whole of Spain disintegrating into anarchy, as had been pretty well universally predicted, it became a parliamentary democracy more or less overnight. Catalonia got regional autonomy and before you could say *busco al vasco bizco brusco* the locals were too rich to work in their own shops. The taxi driver from the airport was some kind of A-rab. This one", he gestured towards the waitress, "is obviously Eastern European. The locals have been allowed to use their own language and now look at the signs – all written in something that is basically Spanish but with the letters removed that would make the words comprehensible. We might as well be in bloody Wales. Nationalism is good but only for as long as it's got a jackboot on its jugular. As soon as it's free to air, it becomes exclusive and oppressive".

Pursey agreed; there was nothing else for it. He didn't much like the place, which was to him a smog bowl filled with greasy food, but it didn't strike him as worth a rant. Baxter continued:

"Another thing: the women. When Spain was under twin constraints – fascism and Roman Catholicism – most English men wouldn't go near the local pussy on the basis that they were wasting their time. But if you made even the slightest effort you could get your end away here much better than in Scandinavia, which had a big reputation as the world shagging centre but in my experience, whenever you tried to get down to it in Stockholm or Oslo, the chicks there only wanted to talk about socialism."

There followed a litany of Baxter's amatory conquests in the land of Velázquez and Lorca. What struck Pursey most forcefully was the banality of it all. That an adult more than halfway through his allotted span should have had sexual congress with some other creature or creatures was scarcely worth remarking: if he'd had four decades of celibacy and hadn't taken holy orders, now that would have been a story.

Baxter was particularly hot on physical descriptions of his conquests. These were either entirely unilluminating – "She had legs up to here and an hourglass figure" – or excessively preoccupied with their bodily hair. If his claims were true, the indigenes must have looked forward to his visits less than those of any Englishman since Sir Francis Drake.

When Jacob Pursey joined Volkmer & Iles, he tried to model himself on Baxter Stratton, but eighteen months on he had come to regard him as no more than a type of salesman, a con artist with insufficient wit to run a scam of his own, a weakling who had panicked over Newnham's royalties.

However, the diminution of Baxter's guru status was also at least partly caused by Pursey's embarrassment at his own tactless remark about Gill Furneaux.

Reviving the subject of the waitress, Pursey said: "Do you think she's blanking us deliberately?"

"No, it's just the great law of continental caffs", said the know-all. "Never serve a punter until he's been sat down for at least a quarter of an hour." He raised his arm and voice, clicked his fingers and called: "*Oiga!*" Having caught the woman's eye, he shouted "*Un hombre se puede morir de sed*'.

The girl came over looking truculent and Stratton asked for dos cervezas.

"Where are you from?" asked Pursey.

"Sabadell," she replied.

"Where's that, Romania?"

"It is a satellite town of Barcelona," said the girl as she wiped the table.

"If you're Espanish…"

"I am Catalan."

"But you speaka Espanish?"

"Of course."

"Did you understand what I just said?"

"I didn't hear you."

"I said *un hombre se puede morir de sed.*"

She turned down her mouth and raised her shoulders.

"But you say you speaka Espanish."

"Yes."

"Yet you don't understand that? Are you sure you're not Polish?"

"No, I told you I am Catalan."

"You must know that expression. *Un hombre*" – and here he threw in a translation for Pursey's benefit – "a man – *se puede* – can – *morir* – die – *de sed* – of thirst."

"I understand the words. I think you mean to say that you are waiting a long time for a drink. But it is maybe an English saying that does not mean the same when you put it into other languages."

"Clever."

"Wait, I bring you your beers."

"Lying through her teeth," said Stratton. "Definitely an illegal."

"Would you?" asked Pursey, fearing he knew the answer.

"Well I certainly wouldn't clamber over her to get to you, old boy."

Later they agreed a distribution deal with Monreal Libros, whose owners seemed pleased with the new arrangement but not so happy that they invited their visitors for dinner. The two Brits thought that a cheek but what can you expect from a race that is never content unless running an auto da fé. They ate together at Los Caracoles, according to Stratton the only restaurant between the Pyrenees and Manhattan. By nine o'clock their attempts at conversation had become so desperate that Baxter was reduced to asking Jake if he knew VI's turnover in Sabadell. At ten, as Barcelona came to life, they agreed they were tired and returned to their hotel. Within an hour they went out again separately and, unknown to each other, ended up in *prostíbulos* less than fifty metres apart on the Ramblas.

§

When George Mascaret got home he found on the doormat a letter from Skidmore inviting him to lunch.

Chapter Three: Around the Houses

The effect on Volkmer & Iles of Clarissa Newnham's discovery of the truth about royalties was similar to that on a pond of a concrete slab dropped from a great height into its middle. At the moment of impact, the first to be discomfited were the big fish in the deep bit; gradually, the waves moved out and rocked lower forms of life in the slime around the banks.

In the primordial biome dwelt the sales representatives, for whom regional weighting was now abolished. Henceforth they were all required to sell equal numbers of every new title. Mick Tettenborn suffered a double blow. First he learned that his target for a book on the Aldeburgh Festival was the same as that set to his counterpart in East Anglia. It was no consolation to him that equal demands were made of them both for a book on the 1952 Lynmouth flood. A bad day in Taunton got worse when the VI credit controller rang to ask him if he had a street map of Cardiff. He didn't, so he was commanded – "I can't help it it's Saturday" – to drive eighty miles from his home to the depths of Wales to buy one. He was then able to inform his masters that the city had no thoroughfare named Sayce Street. Why the question? Because a big invoice thither directed had been returned to VI stamped "Not known". Casing the despatch address in another part of the capital, Mick found a lock-up with storage units let by the week for cash up front.

"Whoever was here has had it away on his toes", the caretaker told him. "You've been fleeced, my friend."

§

London-bound George Mascaret rehearsed answers to the questions he would be asked by his new publishers. Was he available for interview? Unrestrictedly. Would he for that purpose be willing to travel to regional broadcasting studios? With pleasure, but might it be possible for them to pay fares and subsistence? (They could only say no, and he would not have expected any other response, but them as don't ask....) Did he have a CV? In the briefcase.

He then ranged more widely, preparing his responses to the celebrity questionnaires you get in magazines. Favourite food: tournedos Rossini (not that he'd ever had it, but he was sure it would impress the readership of any publication). Biggest influence: on balance, Bob Dylan. What superpower would you like? Invisible scissors with which to cut the wires of obtrusively loud Walkmen in public places.

By "Earliest memory" the real Mascaret was starting to kick in, the George who counted no detail so trivial that it might usefully be omitted from a narrative. The trouble, he said to himself, is that small children have no sense of chronology: how can you reliably tell if the camel ride at the zoo happened before or after the high-speed tricycle collision with the tree stump? Unless your parents tell you, in which case it's reconstruction not genuine recollection. But, reminding himself that journos want answers, not disquisitions on the nature and perception of time, he decided he'd go with the day his house became the last in the street to acquire a telly. It was then he discovered that *Dragnet*, about which he'd previously heard from his classmates, was an L.A. crime drama series, not as he'd imagined a programme about meshing of the kind his English gran wore to keep her hair in place.

With "Favourite writer" he could no longer restrain his instincts. It depends what you mean by "favourite". Some of the authors I love most are bad influences because they exert a gravitational pull on your style but are yet inimitable. Ezra Pound said that the only greats who are safe to read an hour before you start writing are Henry Fielding and Jane Austen. To them I'd add Tobias Smollett.... All right, he replied to a heckle by his reality principle, but no one will know I'm not really entitled to an opinion.

§

Willie Lechler was against change. Which is not to say that he was anti-progress – he was in some ways the most radical member of VI staff. His views were canvassed by junior editors, not because he was their leader but because his perspective was unconventional and sometimes cast solvent light on a wide range of intractable problems, not just those of grammar and syntax; his thoughts were regarded as worth hearing if they were not always practical. And the great thing about him, in the opinion of many, was that he didn't mind if people took his advice or ignored it: he never said "Told you so," a restraint that may be taken as a sign of one who has reached philosophical equilibrium.

Willie Lechler was against change because he doubted that it represented progress; he thought it was more often a sham, a term used as cover for what was seldom more than a changing of the guard. In the words of Pete Townshend, rock star turned publisher, Hyperion turned satyr:

"Meet the new boss

Same as the old boss."

The rise of Jacob Pursey moved Willie first to resentment and shortly thereafter to action. He made up his mind that, if sales low-lifes were going to tell him how to run editorial, he would show them a few things that they ought to be doing but weren't. This was after all a co-operative business.

If marketing initiatives were what they desired, a marketing initiative would be what he'd give them. After heaving and straining awhile, he came up with a new idea for a series that would give a whole load of existing VI books a collective identity. He got a junior in the art department to design a logotype depicting a quill pen clamped in the arms of a woodworking tool and then presented his concept at one of the company's periodical gatherings of senior staff, gatherings that were known as brainstorming sessions until someone objected that that term could be taken as disparaging of the mentally ill.

Thereafter the name got changed to "ideas meetings," which though more politically correct was possibly even less apposite.

"Volkmer & Iles College Editions, to be known by the acronym VICE."

Now in normal discourse, such as for example may take place between friends at dinner parties, it is expected, perhaps even hoped, that a notion such as this will be subjected to a certain amount of scrutiny. Not perhaps the white heat of critical smelting, but reactions and expressions of associated ideas that may hone or pulverise the original. Some may like it; others may be disinterested or even uninterested; there may be those who think it stinks.

Nothing could be further removed from the context of a business meeting, where anything new is greeted with silence as everyone waits for everyone else to set the tone. If the most senior executive approves of it, it would be a brave fool who raised objections in anything other than the most couched and equivocal terms. Conversely, if the honcho hates it, open season will immediately be declared on both idea and inventor.

And what goes for normal firms went a fortiori for this particular publishing house. So when Willie Lechler finished talking, all but one of those present kept quiet and tried to look as if they were thinking it over, like Jack Benny with the mugger who gave him the choice between his money or his life.

But Jake Pursey was at that stage of his career where everyone who mattered agreed with anything he said. He had no need to wait for the reactions of others, so he came straight out with the first thing that popped into his mind.

Willie had anticipated what he thought was the only reasonable objection to his great wheeze, namely that "vice" had overtones or undertones (he was never quite sure of this distinction) of mortal sin. His reply would have been that it riffed on the Volkmer & Iles blue book list, and thus demonstrated that in God's publishing house there are many mansions. "Riffed": the word made him want to throw up his most recent meal, but it was part of the critical and commercial lingua franca.

As a consequence he was entirely unprepared for Pursey's comment, which was:

"The Yanks spell vice with an 'S'."

And so indeed they do; there was no gainsaying it; then began a crescendo of vocal disapproval which Willie tried to silence by saying:

"I should point out that these books are sold exclusively in current and former Commonwealth countries; we don't have rights in the USA or Canada."

But Baxter Stratton backed his boy.

"I'm sorry, Willie, this really won't wash."

Willie shrugged. He had based the whole concept on the premise that anything he thought was stupid would be welcomed by fools, so this response did a little to restore his faith in their taste and discernment. He thought "You cannot, sir, take from me anything that I will more willingly part withal" and, even though he didn't actually say that, he was so pleased to have come up with such an apposite quotation at the perfect moment – which he knew was much more difficult than making an original remark – that he paid no heed to the possible consequences of letting go of the tiger's tail.

§

Behind Skidmore's clean, modern reception area drooped an office with a range of manuscript peaks and printout sierras on almost every floor tile. The walkway between the papers looked as if it had to be dredged every morning to keep it open. On the shelves were dusty reference books with dependent cobwebs, like a schooner's rigging. On the desks were Bakelite phones that would have enthused the properties manager of a Pinero revival and typewriters with rusty golf balls that looked as if they had only recently been salvaged from the water hazards in which they had lain since being hooked there by Sam Snead.

If the place was a port, it wasn't in a warm latitude. As George Mascaret approached under his own steam the only woman in the room who was scrubbed up and dressed like she was about to meet an author, her colleagues glanced at him furtively and disapprovingly, as if he were the gunboat of some colonial power. He imagined them feeling under the desks for their ice picks.

Robin Peppiatt was little friendlier.

"You're early."

He always was and he had a quip for those who pointed it out to him.

"Punctuality is the courtesy of kings, but I aim even higher."

It didn't go down well. It never did. He wondered why he kept using it.

Robin said, "I'll see if the others are ready", then walked into a glass-panelled office and spoke to a sweaty endomorph in a polo shirt who immediately started scrabbling through manuscripts. Failing to find what he was looking for, he continued his search in a state of mounting agitation. Robin disappeared into another room and re-emerged a minute later with a mantis-like geezer who introduced himself as "Marcus the publisher". George wondered whether that should be written with a lower case p or a capital, as in Lily the Pink.

The three of them stood in silence and watched the endomorph until he made a histrionic eureka gesture and came out clutching triumphantly the right sheaf of A4.

On the way to a nearby wine bar George gave them an account of his journey to London that took in every station to Balham but then, in response to an apparent lack of audience engagement, went non-stop to Charing Cross and omitted altogether the bus on which he completed the final stage.

Surveying the menu he fancied the scallops to start and the paella as a main course but, when Marcus the publisher ordered pâté and toast, the endomorph chose hummus and pitta and Robin went for the vegetarian meze, he twigged that he was dining with cheese-parers and restricted himself to the cheapest item, the soup of the day, French onion, which he couldn't stand.

Having divided the contents of a carafe of house red into four little Duralex glasses, Marcus the publisher told George what was on his mind.

"We've all read *101 Reasons for Staying Single* and we have a number of concerns."

Opening the manuscript, the endomorph continued: "There are several topics that we don't agree are cogent reasons for not getting married."

Mascaret looked at Robin, who had approved his list, but she kept her eyes fixed on the tabletop.

"Take point fourteen under the heading 'You don't have to have opinions.' There you say: 'In any normal relationship – i.e., one unconstrained by sex and finance – each partner is at perfect liberty to disagree with the other', setra setra."

"Setra setra?" thought Mascaret.

"You go on to give examples of occasions when husbands and wives agree with each other in the interests of a quiet life. These are perfectly well written and quite funny in their way…"

"In their way?" said Mascaret.

"But they don't tell the whole story. The picture is incomplete," put in Marcus the publisher. "We've identified several other instances."

On cue the endomorph turned to another of the pages flagged with yellow Post-it notes and said:

"Point twenty-four: 'You don't have to pretend to like sloppy films if you're a man or Formula One motor racing if you're a woman'. This entry begins: 'Insofar as it is possible to generalise, most heterosexual men take the view that *The Sound of Music* is too long and sentimental. When they get together, the joke that the film is to be remade with a happy ending in which the Nazis catch the von Trapp family is so canonical that it hardly needs retelling'."

George always wrote in the hope of one day being quoted; now the time had come, he felt like a convict hearing his previous read out in court by the beak. It struck him that, if a story doesn't need retelling, why retell it, but that wasn't the point they were trying to make.

"You see we're both heterosexual males," said Marcus the p, exchanging a virile glance with the endomorph, "and we've never heard that".

"So you've learned something; the reader's learned something," said George.

"Perhaps, but it makes the work factional rather than universal."

"Could not the same be said of all books?"

Ignoring that, M the p went off on another one.

"And there are stylistic difficulties."

At this portentous phrase George thought "How smart a lash that speech doth give my conscience"; again the endomorph referred to the text.

"You describe something as 'a metaphor of' when it should be 'a metaphor for'."

This was not among the errors George had identified after submitting the text.

"I've always thought that 'metaphor for' has an ugly echo – 'phor' and 'for' right up close together."

"But it's not what people say."

"They might adopt it once it has the authority of my usage."

Some throat-clearing, then:

"There's a bit in point seventy-nine where you say: 'One of the features that make this approach hard to define', setra setra…"

"Setra setra," said Mascaret sardonically.

"It should be 'one of the features that makes this approach hard to define'."

"Well I'm not so sure my version is wrong, but if it is, is that not something the desk editor should deal with?"

Mascaret addressed this to the one he assumed would be taking that role, but this was a robin in name only: at the table she made like the dumbest of mute swans.

"The difficulty is, George," said Marcus the publisher, "we no longer have any confidence that we can sell this book. We want to withdraw it from our list".

Mascaret looked hellish volumes.

"I'm very sorry. If it's any consolation, as you've done all the work we won't be asking for the advance back."

George thought "Fuckin' a-right you won't", but he said: "Well I suppose in the circumstances that's the best I can hope for." He added that it was a pity and they all agreed with him.

§

"Editorial is the ideas powerhouse of any publishing company."

"That's bollocks. Editorial is an adjunct of production."

Thus concluded the meeting at which Baxter Stratton revealed to Willy Lechler his plans for "replumbing the organisation." These included making Minie and Homo redundant and handing over half of the new commissioning to the sales department. Willy could keep the academic list, but trade books – the ones that were meant to be popular – were henceforth to be within the purview of Jacob Pursey.

§

Through the seven previous novels Clarissa Newnham had established herself in a niche that was not so much thematic – her work ranged widely through reimagined memoir, thriller and historical romance – as taxonomical. She was often described as being in a class of her own, a term conventionally applied to nonpareils but which here alluded to the difficulty of categorising her as anything. Which might have made her an object of fascination, but while professional critics were unanimous – or at least unwilling to dispute the proposition –

that she was good, it seemed that they would rather praise her than read her. At least, that was what might have been surmised from reviews of *Behind A Dream*, which came out in dribs and drabs over the quarter that followed the work's appearance in bookshops. None of the write-ups was longer than five hundred words; most were laudatory snippets that made no attempt to grapple with structure, plot, use of language or any of the other matters that academic critics might be expected to address. If they ever had turned their attention to the minutiae they might have found some fault with Newnham's idea of local colour, which was seldom more than descriptions that could have been lifted from street maps: "Slow for the lights at the intersection after Ku'Damm, then left into Unter Den Linden." They might also have had something to say about purple passages that gave readers such plums as "impartial sun," "judgemental moon" and "clamorous acne." Of the few reviews that didn't paraphrase VI's own blurb, the highest praise appeared in *The Sunday Times*, whose woman liked – or affected to like – Newnham's "ballsy high-octane prose." *The Mail on Sunday* called it "a breath of fresh air," but made no cost comparison between the VI hardback and a walk on a heath; the *Guardian* admired the author's "Shakespearean vision," a phrase doubtless inspired by recognition of the source of the title; if it was based on a close reading of the text, there was no supporting evidence.

§

When Jacob Pursey took over the VI slush pile he feared that it would be full of books like James Cree's memoirs. He was pleasantly surprised to find that most of the unsolicited manuscripts were works of fiction that seldom took up more than two hundred pages of A4 and could be judged in the first couple of paragraphs, which by a genial coincidence was about his attention span.

The publishing decisions were his alone; the committee to which Willy Lechler had referred now convened only for academic books. Pursey was not so arrogant as to spurn advice; he once even sought it on a visit to W.H. Smith's head office in Swindon. But what he thought was a searching question – "What would really sell?" – elicited from the chief buyer the quick-as-a-flash response "A how-to book on converting base metal into gold". This was too vatic for Pursey's purposes, and thenceforth he relied exclusively on instinct.

To put his own stamp on the selection process, Pursey abandoned VI's stereotyped slip and wrote personal letters to the hopeful authors he was disappointing.

Rejection was naturally the fate of most submissions, but among the books Pursey signed up was a children's adventure story that would become an international best-seller and be turned into a Hollywood film. He later claimed that its genius jumped off the page at him and that he'd found it unputdownable, a real page-turner. In truth, his wheels had spun in the mud of the third sentence; what tipped the critical balance was the willingness expressed by the author, a single mother, in her covering letter to put her life savings towards the initial printing costs.

After a few months, Pursey realised his original idea – that there were only two kinds of book, those he commissioned and those he turned down – was simplistic. He now identified a third, more dangerous category – scripts that having been rejected by him found favour and success elsewhere. He decided that he needed a 2-I-C. He appealed to Baxter Stratton, who agreed in principle but reminded him that there was no money to hire and the roster of sub-editors had already been halved. They agreed that they couldn't ask Willie because he'd give them a rich mouthful followed by a claim for constructive dismissal. It didn't take them much more than one bottle to identify the ideal candidate to take the strain. As Pursey the Elder had said, work migrates to those who can do it.

§

Leaving the wine bar, Marcus the publisher and the endomorph walked on ahead; the Robin lighted on George's wrist and at last began to sing.

"Don't feel too badly."

"That's quite hard at the moment."

"There's nothing wrong with your book. Their criticisms were designed to throw you. The real reason they've got cold feet is they want celebrity authors and you're not famous."

And then more courtesy as afterthought:

"At least, not as famous as the Duchess of York, who might be doing a travel book for us. She's all they ever talk about at the moment."

This was revealing but there was nothing George could do about it. If he accelerated and put it to the two men in front it would merely get his informant into trouble. If he mounted a defence, pointing out that he hadn't misrepresented himself – he was as famous today as he had been when Skidmore approached him in the first place – he might score debating points but he still wouldn't get his book published. So he said nothing and soon decided that it would have been better to remain unenlightened. As he later reflected in his Journal: "All knowledge is debilitating".

§

"I never went looking for an editorial remit, but having agreed to it I've really enjoyed myself. Although self-praise is no recommendation, I have to say that I'm proud of what I've achieved. But in success lie the seeds of failure, which can always sprout unless you're very careful. None of us, not even Gill Furneaux, foresaw how rapid growth would be under the new dispensation. As sales increase – in fact, they're shooting off the graph – that's more work for me, and as we attract more authors, that's more work for me as well. So we tried to identify someone who could help me sort the wheat from the chaff, and yours was the name that kept coming up."

Pursey didn't prepare this spiel, through a combination of sloth and the desire to retain spontaneity. There were parts of it that he knew the listener would divine were untrue, but the falsehoods were unsusceptible of proof. And both parties knew that it wasn't really an offer, it was a gift-wrapped instruction. Like it or not, from now on the addressee was going to be working for him.

The chosen one could not help noticing that Pursey made no mention of a pay rise, but everyone at VI knew that money was king only insofar as it was not a subject. On the plus side, she loved reading and had long been frustrated by lack of opportunity to put her bookishness to productive use.

So Ella accepted and Jake told her that was very good news.

"You know, I remember you telling me you had a sister, but you never said you were twins."

"You never asked."

"Identical?"

Ella nodded; she felt with a tinge of sadness that she knew what was coming.

"I'd really like to meet her."

"One day, maybe; next time she's around."

"How about dinner tonight? To celebrate."

"Sorry, no. I'm going on holiday tomorrow; I've got to pack."

"Heigh-ho, never mind. There'll be other times. We'll start you off as soon as you get back, yes?"

§

When George Mascaret felt tired at inapt moments he knew that he ought to do something physical but he never could quite get his tracksuit on before falling asleep in the armchair in his study. Whenever thwarted professionally he would decide to pack in the inky trade and retrain as a landscape gardener or take up something else that didn't interest him but which might be in some unfocused sense improving and could hardly be less remunerative than his current line.

But age was against him. In his twenties he had pulled the face of an editor-cum-writer and when the wind changed he couldn't straighten out his features. He was reminded of two entries in his commonplace book, which was uniform in series with the Journal and lay next to it on his desk. One was a short extract from *The Little Genius*, Mervyn Horder's memoir of his father: "In many cases where boys have a strong desire for a special calling, it is more a whim than fitness that lies at the bottom of their choice". The other was: "Be careful what you want, young man, for you will surely get it." When quoting this to his children he told them it was Emerson because it was to Emerson that the remark was attributed in *A Texan in England*. He'd never located the original source, not that he'd looked very hard, and sometimes wondered if it might have been J. Frank Dobie, author of said work, giving Harvard airs to a crack of his own.

Normally George had no difficulty with rejection: he could

accept that he had been found wanting as long as he knew he'd been weighed on accurate scales. But lunch with Skidmore had been a grievous thwart. He felt he was the injured party, and righteous indignation inspired a brief flurry of proactivity during which he made multiple photocopies of the rejected script and sent a set of each to a dozen publishers. These included the usual suspects – Wilby Bestsellers, The Clifford Press and the Denver shower, who had a trade imprint as well as an academic arm.

§

Ella spent her week off in a cottage on the edge of a fjord. Bergen had been her first solo foreign destination – as a student she had seen, read and loved *A Doll's House* and for a few months entertained a notion that she would learn the language in which it was written and produce a better English translation of the play than William Archer's or Michael Meyer's. That plan was soon abandoned but the trip produced what she called her first proper boyfriend. After a brief summer fling they kept in contact by letter and she saw him every time she returned to Norway.

Over the next two decades, Hakon had changed from her image of the perfect Viking – tall, blond, gentle and literary – into a stooped, balding cardigan-wearer with pipe-smoker's teeth. His marriage might have signalled the end of their friendship but Kari welcomed Ella on her biennial visits to their home.

It was by Hakon's physical ageing that Ella measured her own course through the Vale of Tears. She still looked much as she had at twenty; the lines on her face were deepening, but slowly, and they were still easily concealable with cosmetics. His career, though by no means meteoric, had consistently described an upward arc – a doctorate in history, a job as a librarian, a decent marriage. That she mildly envied his success was an effect of her own low status and self-esteem: the editorial brief she'd just been handed was the closest to promotion she'd had in a decade. And she was on the cusp of transition from "single" to "spinster".

One evening after dinner the three of them were sitting on the deck, the Norwegians gazing at the mountains, Ella just loving the sky, when she asked after Ulf.

Through his reading, Hakon had become preoccupied with the idea that the only children who succeed in life are those whose fathers are deceased, negligent or absent. Unable to grant his son two of these benisons he contrived the third by sending him away to a private school in Newcastle. There the boy became more English than Blake's Jerusalem, notwithstanding that he was forever known to his classmates as Nog, and caught the boat home with diminishing frequency: in his first year he'd come back at the end of every term; now that he was fifteen, his parents had to fight for him at Christmas.

"Every day without Ulf hurts Kari and me, but what weakens us strengthens him. It also gives us reasons and excuses to visit England."

"But only the North," said Ella.

"We always mean to come to London, but we have you there as our special correspondent. How is the centre of the British Empire?"

"Constantly altering yet oddly unchanging. Dirty, tiring and too expensive even for someone on fifty per cent more than the national average income. I'd like to buy a flat, but I'll never be able to."

"Is it not possible to pool resources with someone else? Your sister?"

"We haven't spoken since mother died."

"That's sad," said Kari.

"If people are kind, it's good to have them around; if they're poisonous, it's good not to. The only problem I have with our relationship is telling people about it. Everyone expects us to conform to the stereotypes they've read about twins in magazines. Telepathic rapport: if she stubs her toe in Stockport, I writhe in Rochdale. If I snog a bloke in Baltimore, she gets love bites on her neck in Nairobi. If I had a pound for every time I've been asked if we have our own private language, I'd be able to afford a deposit just like that. But we don't and as far as I can remember we never did. Most women think it must be hard for the two of us to form relationships with other people, a presumption based on the idea that, since we were together in the womb, the other one is all we ever need. Some men get very excited to learn that I'm a twin and seem to think they might be able to wangle themselves some hot three-in-a-bed full-on lesbo action."

Hakon and Kari did not fully understand the last sentence but they got the drift well enough to look glum.

That night in bed Ella read a couple of pages of Hanna Astrup Larsen's biography of Knut Hamsun before turning to the *Private Eye* she'd bought on her way to the airport. In the magazine's Literary Review section she found the following:

"In a bungle that looks big even by the standards of the book trade, Volkmer & Iles have turned down *The Catcher in the Rye* a quarter of a century after it became an international best-seller.

"Having received numerous rejections of his own work from a host of publishers and agents, aspiring novelist Taylor Henshaw (who works by day for the Central Office of Information) typed out the first three chapters of J.D. Salinger's masterpiece and submitted them under an assumed name to the Fitzrovia-based firm.

"The work begins: 'If you really want to hear about it, the first thing you'll probably want to know is where I was born, and what my lousy childhood was like, and how my parents were occupied and all before they had me, and all that David Copperfield kind of crap, but I don't feel like going into it'.

"Since the book's original publication in 1951, this has become one of the most famous openings in English literature but it is evidently not so well known that it has come to the attention of VI, who rejected the work on the grounds that it was 'too obviously derivative from Charles Dickens'. And who took this momentous decision? Step forward sales manager

Jacob Pursey, aka CAUC, an acronym of 'Complete And Utter Cunt'. If CAUC picks the books, what one wonders does editorial director (amiable lettuce leaf Big 'Willie' Lechler) do: the MD's typing?"

Oh dear, thought Ella, silly Jake; poor Jake; perhaps only I can save him.

§

In the good old days at Wilby Bestsellers, Jez Yaxley cascaded unsolicited manuscripts to his sub-editors, but after they were sacrificed to the new economic austerity and he had to take up all their fardels in addition to his own he normally left the works lying around until the authors started chasing, whereupon he returned them unread with a cursory note.

101 Reasons for Staying Single was an exception, however, because there was nothing Jake wanted less than a follow-up call from the sender.

Reading bits of the work, though, he decided that style may not after all be the man himself. Because although it was mannered it wasn't prolix and although it wasn't riveting it demonstrated a lightness of tone that was notably absent from the author's conversation. Jez supposed that was why writers wrote – because they couldn't, for whatever reason, get and hold people's attention any other way. Who would go to the trouble of committing their thoughts to paper when it's so much easier to talk?

"In any normal relationship – that is to say, one unconstrained by sex and finance – each partner is at perfect liberty to disagree with the other. If, to adapt a classic example from Evelyn Waugh's *Scoop*, one person says that the capital of Japan is Yokohama, the other may raise a point of information without causing offence.

"Not so in marriage. In that honourable estate, every assertion – be it ne'er so groundless – is a power play. If you are the one whose grasp of geography is flimsier than that of Lord Copper, your display of ignorance has created a situation: if your partner agrees with you, you're right; if he or she keeps shtum, you can later blame him or her for not having drawn attention to your mistake at once; if you are corrected, don't stand for it because to do so would be a loss of face.

"In a perfectly civilised world, there are no disputes about matters of fact; in the real one... a friend once told me that he and his colleagues had spent an afternoon (on full pay) 'discussing where St Johnstone [the mid-ranking Scottish football team] is'. 'Discussing' defies satire.

"And when it comes to matters of opinion, how many participants in long-term sexual relationships can ever admit to their partners that they don't know what they think? 'I don't really have a favourite novel' – incendiary; 'I'm not sure if Pavarotti is better than Carreras' – sedition; 'I don't know if I'm left-wing or right-wing' – grounds for separation".

But one of the two or three things that Jez Yaxley knew for certain was that the quality of a book had about as much bearing on the decision to publish as the Norman Conquest had on Cuba. If good writing was the sole or even a criterion, poets would have chauffeurs.

§

The man on the check-in desk at Oslo Airport took an interest in Ella's surname. As he reached for the LHR luggage tag he said:

"I used to live in Bethune Road in London."

"Some people pronounce it 'Beeton'."

"Like Mrs Beeton, your English cook."

"I always think it should be 'beaten' as in 'defeated' myself", said Ella. She sometimes found herself revealing more to strangers than she would to her closest intimates. "But you were right the first time; we just say it as it's spelt."

As she walked to security she decided that the Nordic gloom had got to her and it was as well she was going home.

§

After interviewing a string of duds, Marcus the publisher suddenly got the feeling that Candidate Seven might be just what he was looking for.

"Why did you decide to leave your last job?"

"I can't really say that I decided any such thing. They told me I was superfluous to requirements."

Honesty: a quality Marcus admired in other people.

"I've heard they're difficult to work for."

"Not really; I had five good years."

Tact and the ability to maintain a brave face even when it was being hosed with ordure: two more boxes ticked.

"And what was your final salary there?"

Marcus liked the answer to this, too: the applicant had evidently avoided the error of pricing himself out of the market.

"This is an immediate vacancy. We need someone who can start right away so that he or she can pick up the reins from Robin Peppiatt, who's had an offer she can't refuse from Weidenfeld and is leaving at the end of the month." That much was true. Then he added: "She's been a good and loyal servant. We wish her well."

"Obviously in the circumstances, that wouldn't be a problem for me."

And so saying, Colin Dodd began the reconstruction of what he was pleased to call his career. He sloughed his old identity, Minie the Sub, and began styling himself "Publishing Director".

§

Ciaran Addey rang to say that *101 Reasons* was not for him but wondered if George might like to turn out for The Clifford Press in their annual game against Columbus Books.

George said he'd get back to him after he'd checked the family diary, by which he meant engaged Vivienne in a discussion of the pros and cons of playing for the first time in three years without any practice.

"You might get some work out of it."

"Yes, if I make a quick 40, take three for 17 and hold a couple of blinding catches, but the greater likelihood is that I'll be useless and they'll all think I work like I play."

"What would you do otherwise? Sit in the study and fester about Skidmark? Go on, get in amongst them. Whatever happened to George Mascaret, man of action?"

"He's lying in the bottom of a drawer under my whites."

"If he brings them down his doting helpmate may wash them."

§

To ensure that no interested or involved party missed the *Private Eye* piece, someone, presumably the author or the source of the information (assuming they were not the same person), posted them each a photocopy of the page. Gill Furneaux was relaxed about hers. She reminded Baxter Stratton that all publicity was good publicity, but he, also uncharacteristically, took the view that something must be done. He arrived at this conclusion after showing his copy to Willie Lechler, who immediately produced from his pocket an identical mail shot addressed to him in the same disguised hand.

"Which proves he wrote it", Baxter told Gill.

"How do you work that out?"

"Why else would he carry it with him all the time?"

"For the same reason you do. Perhaps he just happened to have it on him. Anyway, he would hardly describe himself as a lettuce leaf."

"Of course he would, to throw us off the scent."

Baxter summoned Jake.

"This doesn't just make us look like CAUCs, it makes us look like ignorant CAUCs."

"Me, you mean."

"The whole firm."

"Look, Bax, you can't micromanage editorial. I can't double-check everything that Ella reads."

Baxter noted how useful Ella had already become in her new job, even before she'd started it. In Pursey's place he'd no doubt have made the same move, but he still found it difficult to admire.

"All the letters go out under your name."

"How do you expect me to sign them? Max Volkmer? Or Harold Iles, maybe I could get away with Harold Iles."

Fuck it, thought Jake, that was a damn fool thing to say, a violation of paternal precept three, the one about never using reductio ad absurdum to illustrate a point. Asking for trouble. In an effort to retrieve the situation he added:

"If I'd had any idea that this would be how you'd react I'd have come here with the *Encyclopedia Britannica* stuck down the back of my trousers."

"You're missing the point. What I mean is, when you're choosing books you can't go calling yourself sales manager."

Jake didn't like the sound of this at all: he wasn't sure that he had ever needed wiseacre tips from this over-promoted nobody but if he had the time was past.

"What are you suggesting?"

Baxter Stratton noted the tone of hostility. Knowing that he could hardly sack someone he'd so recently promoted, he switched to unctuous.

"Simply that you use a more appropriate title."

"Such as?"

"I've thought about this." He hadn't. "What about editor in chief?"

Jake relaxed a bit but remained on the lookout for gin traps.

"I do the same job, though, both prongs?"

"Yes, of course both prongs", said Baxter, thinking Hell yes, you don't imagine I'd do any of it, do you?

"So I'd be sales manager when dealing with sales and editor in chief when dealing with authors?"

"Exactly."

"Sounds good to me", said Jake, back at ease now and thinking that Teflon Cy was after all a much more apposite nickname than CAUC. "But won't that piss Willie off?"

"Who knows?" said Baxter. "Maybe it will. We'll just have to live with the pain."

§

On an overcast day at a ground in the middle of nowhere, Norfolk, Columbus won the toss and elected to bat. That suited Ciaran Addey, who would have put them in anyway to ensure that the game didn't end before teatime. Four of his XI he'd never met – they were friends of colleagues. George and two others were freelances he knew slightly but had never seen play. Although he punctiliously asked them on arrival what they did, all but one of them said what cricketers say in such circs – "Bat a bit, bowl a bit", a spectral cocktail of modesty and conceit that casts less light on their abilities than a blackout curtain. The sole exception, George Mascaret said he would do whatever the captain wanted him to do.

The first few overs were tight. The openers played and missed at a South African medium pacer – blond, with a gold cap on one of his front teeth, an Apartheid dreamboat who moved the ball both ways off the seam – and a left-armer in a *patka* who bowled what might have been identified as rubbish had he not diverted attention from its true nature with pre-delivery hocus-pocus in which he bounced the ball off his forearm into one hand and then spun it into the other before running in around the wicket and bringing his arm over so low that at the moment of release his hand was almost level with his shoulder.

After six overs with the score having just reached double figures, No. 1 opened his shoulders for the first time and played an off-drive. He didn't really get hold of it, but there was an easy single – mid-off was deep and not that interested. George moved from cover and bent to field the ball one-handed. He got down to it all right, but he noticed that his swoop, which twenty years previously he had described as an action that could be performed only by the product of a union between Colin Bland and a sea eagle, was now impaired by a paunch that he could no longer veraciously describe as incipient. As he underarmed the ball back to the bowler, who had taken up position behind the stumps, he fell on this newly discovered mound with a thud that he feared might be audible in King's Lynn. Winded, he was glad when, later in the innings as the field spread out, he was repositioned at long leg and deep extra.

There he grazed until the fall of the sixth wicket half an hour before tea. Ciaran asked him if he fancied the next over from the other end. There were few activities that George enjoyed more than bowling, but since he hadn't turned his arm over for about five years since he last played with Hector, he was afraid of making a fool of himself. But it seemed a shame to come all this way and not make the best of it, so he handed his sweater to the umpire and measured out a seven-pace run.

The first ball was slow and tame but deliberate to make sure that he could still pitch the bloody thing on the wicket. It wanted hitting, but the nervous new batsman just patted it back along the pitch.

To the second ball Mascaret applied some spin by bringing it out of the back of his hand and twisting his wrist at the moment of release. It turned a bit, but it was short and wide of the leg stump so the batsman slogged it to the boundary, which it crossed just after bouncing.

For the third delivery he repeated the action but made no attempt to spin the ball, instead tossing it up a bit higher from behind the popping crease. This was the variation that had sometimes brought him wickets in his youth but more often put the fear of God into anyone mad enough to field in a catching position in front of the wicket. The batsman shaped to swing but, realising he'd misjudged the flight, settled for an awkward-looking cross-bat forward defensive.

As George walked back to his mark he decided that the next one would be the quicker ball. In the delivery stride he bent his back but he let go too early, before his arm had brushed his ear.

The ball arced in a gentle parabola. The batsman thought about giving it the treatment but it reached him at nose height so he dropped his head and let it go through to the wicketkeeper.

George raised his hand but before he could apologise the umpire turned towards the scorebox, held out his arm and called "No ball". This was a literalist interpretation, but nothing like as harsh as the next thing he said: "Law 42: intimidatory bowling. One more of them and you're off".

The last three balls were wide of off stump and the batsman, rattled, left them alone. At the end of the over there was no applause; no one said "Well bowled"; there was just embarrassed silence. As George trotted off into the deep he predicted, correctly, that he would not be asked to bowl again: he would be remembered by twenty-one potential sources of income (more if you counted the small crowd on the steps of the pavilion) as the man who tried to decapitate an opponent in a friendly.

§

On the plane home, Ella got talking to the passenger next to her, an American who, like a character in *My Life and Loves* by Frank Harris, needed no nudging to spill every bean of her back story. As she listened to the early stages of this woman's monologue, Ella felt like pointing out that buttonholing strangers and subjecting them to a word torrent which made the Ancient Mariner seem taciturn and succinct might play well over the contiguous forty-eight, but throughout Britain, and even on flights to and from the sceptred isle, it was regarded as something of a lapse in taste. But gradually polite restraint turned to fascination. Her name was Jan Hoffmann. She had fled Germany in the Thirties for the usual reasons and pitched up in New York. When the United States entered the Second World War she was recruited to lead a special service unit whose secret mission was to infiltrate Norway and assassinate the Nazi puppet ruler Vidkun Quisling. She had reported only to President Roosevelt. The group of four – herself and three Norwegian resistance fighters – had come within a whisker of completing their assignment, but the plot was foiled when the one detailed to leave the briefcase with the bomb under the leader's desk was searched on his way into the meeting room. He was shot and the others melted into the mountains, where they lived rough until the end of the conflict. Jan Hoffmann had just been to see Paul, one of the other members. He was terminally ill, so it was a valediction. They spent their time together trying to solve the mystery of the mission: had they been betrayed, and if so by whom?

§

Columbus declared on 193 for 7. During the tea interval, Ciaran Addey decided the Clifford batting order. He put himself at eight, his regulars at one, two and three, and then asked George to bat four. This was courteous, since George had driven further than anyone else and at short notice. And good captaincy, which George had rarely encountered: he had given up playing regularly after the second time he'd turned out once for an established team and then fielded at deep fine leg at both ends, never been asked to bowl, and put in at No. 11.

As The Clifford Press began their reply, George occupied a centrally located deckchair and got ready to network. He'd just started talking to the South African when out in the middle there was a clunk of bails as the opener was castled fourth ball.

No. 3 hurriedly put on his gloves and began the walk to the wicket. As the next man in George now had to get ready too: he could be needed at any minute.

In the Stygian dressing room he was alone. He positioned his box and then put on his pads, struggling with the straps because his hands were trembling. The bootlaces were no easier. He then made the first of several visits to the lavatory, which here was not the kind of amenity you'd dream of using unless you had to. And all the time he kept his ears peeled for the cries of exultant fielders.

When he came back outside his mouth was so dry that he spoke to none of the other players; he just watched the match with a level of attention of which he had forgotten himself capable. Even the most trivial on-field occurrence assumed momentous significance. If the batsmen played and missed, George felt the surge of adrenaline and the liquefaction of the bowel. With every lofted shot, the yells of "Catch it" made him half rise from his chair. There was no two so easy that he didn't think they should have contented themselves with a single, no single so safe that he did not whisper to himself either "No, no, wait on" or "Careful, he's got an arm". The pauses between *howzats* and *not outs* seemed to him longer than gaps in the fossil record.

An impartial observer with a comparably obsessional level of interest in on-field proceedings might have pointed out that the bowling wasn't up to much and the batsmen were comfortably in control, especially after they'd both passed 50. But if such a person was present, he wasn't making his views known to George, who was so intent on the minutiae that he failed to see the bigger picture. When No. 3, going for his century, took a mighty swing at a well pitched up ball and was caught at midwicket, the incoming batsman had no idea until he checked the scoreboard that the sides were now level.

On reaching the crease, George placed his bat in position and asked for middle and leg.

"That is two legs", said the umpire who'd called him for the beamer. "Right arm over; two to come."

"Dunno why tha's botherin' t' take guard," said the wicketkeeper. "Ye'll not be 'ere that long. Mine you, that's wha' I said to t' last bloke." The slips laughed like a claque.

George still couldn't speak, which was probably just as well because if he'd said what he had in mind – "Shut up, you twot, this is hard enough as it is without having to listen to your heavily stylised regional drivel; can't you see I'm trying to concentrate?" – he might have caused another incident.

There followed a brief delay while the Columbus captain brought all his men in to save the single – a futile move when there's one to get in half an hour with eight wickets in hand, but that's what always happens at such a point in any match.

Finally the bowler began his approach. His fifteen pace run-up didn't take long but it was time enough for George to think many things. About how this was simultaneously the perfect hand and the hospital pass. If he hit the ball out of the ground, he would savour the moment for ever. But while everyone present might recall the result, only he would remember who'd sealed the victory. The match-winning partnership would be venerated in the annals of The Clifford Press; they might even produce a commemorative booklet. And the opener who got a duck would never be allowed to forget that he'd missed out. But the winning hit and the player who made it would not merit so much as a footnote. He would be the never-to-be-invited-back guest who tried to maim some poor mite from the

Columbus warehouse who hadn't picked up a bat since primary school. And then of course there was the worst-case scenario: he might get out and thus become the man who came in needing one to win and couldn't even manage that.

So while the fielders were joking among themselves and the non-striker took off his gloves to facilitate a "set 'em up, mine's a pint" gesture to the bartender, a cloud of impending doom hung over George Mascaret.

The ball pitched half way down the wicket and swung away to leg. George swiped at it but missed. The umpire stared long and hard and began to raise his arms to indicate a wide but then, remembering his earlier pedantry and the state of the game, thought better of it and put them down again.

"Bowl on t'wicket, Howard", said the keeper, "else we'll be here all bastard night".

Howard collected the ball and walked back, but this time he went on a good ten yards beyond his mark. The keeper retreated a step or two as well, and said to George as he was doing so: "Ah trust tha's wearin' adequate proh-tection".

The build-up was different but the ball that then arrived was almost the same as the one before. George swung anticlockwise from his stance at noon until he hit the ball at about seven o'clock, then followed through so far that it sailed over the slips and crossed the boundary, not backward of square on the leg side as prescribed in the textbooks, but over third man.

"Bit streaky that, weren't it?" said the keeper as they all trooped off.

§

As the plane followed the line of the Thames upstream towards Hounslow, Jan Hoffmann and Ella exchanged business cards.

"You're in the book world? I knew it! Listen," said Jan Hoffmann, as if that wasn't what Ella had been doing from the moment the undercarriage retracted, "I've written a memoir. A lot of the details are still classified information, but it does give a unique insight into my relationship with FDR. Would you…?"

"I'm not the person who takes the publishing decisions", said Ella, and having said it she wondered if it would have been unwise to have added "yet". "But I'd certainly like to take a look if you were willing to send it along."

"I'm not interested in money; any advance I might receive would be given straight to charity. All I want is for the story to be told and out there."

At Terminal Two their paths diverged: Ella Bethune's towards the baggage reclaim, Jan Hoffmann's to a connecting flight to Newark.

§

On the drive home from the match, George Mascaret's mind cast off again onto the ocean of fire. If cricket is the image of existence, what detailed parallels were to be drawn from his part in today's eight-wicket victory? He had suffered injustice –

thanks to the officious arse in the white coat his innocuous leg-breaks would be spoken of in the same breath as the fastest and most suspect deliveries of Charlie Griffith – so that was consistent with both recent experience and eternal verity. He had had a moment of glory, but it was a long time coming. And although in years to come he would no doubt talk up his decisive swing of the bat – G.L. Mascaret not out 6 – the truth was that anyone could have done the same if he'd happened to be there: success, if that's what you call it, is largely about being in the right place at the right time.

And that he'd failed to establish any contacts with potential employers also struck him as life in little. He thought of the numerous times he'd observed his children in the garden. The notion that they ever played together was plainly misconceived: while Hector was building castles in the sandpit, Charley would be moving water from one plastic bucket to another and Agnes would be making daisy chains. They were in each other's company and yet alone, just as they entered the world and just as they would leave it.

As he pulled down the windscreen visor to shield his eyes from the evening sun he further thought that the pathetic fallacy was a load of cock, literature's way of reminding readers that it wasn't verisimilar, it wasn't even slightly similar. If it was there would at that moment have been hurricanoes and torrential rain.

§

Back in harness by day Ella continued as publicity manager; in the evenings and at weekends she waded through the slush pile. At first she counted herself one of the luckiest people alive: her critical judgments were no longer mere breeze-shooting; they had commercial consequences; she held the power of publishing.

Her new responsibilities confirmed her long-held belief that she could reliably identify within the first ten pages whether a book had merit. Although she had always made it a point of honour to finish reading everything she began, she now felt she had to keep going to the end of each submission, if only in order to adduce cogent reasons for rejecting it. This obligation – which was entirely self-imposed; she knew no other professional reader who would have gone to so much trouble – became increasingly onerous. She worried that the long hours would so desensitise her that, in the unlikely event of her encountering a talent, she would not see the light for the bushel. It was not long before her enthusiasm was snuffed out by the sheer volume of dross with which she was inundated: most of the material was an affront to the memory of the trees that had died in its creation.

Once she'd stopped enjoying herself, the iniquities of her situation began to rankle. In her first six months she read one hundred books. Of the five she considered worth bringing to the attention of the editor in chief, not one was signed up.

When she complained, Jake offered her a finder's fee of fifty pounds for every book earmarked by her that made it into published form. This was no big deal, but he was keen to keep her onside so that she would carry on generating letters like:

Dear Mr Grylls

Thank you so much for giving us the opportunity to read *The Private Diary of Montague Dawson, Flagellant.*

Your novel divided opinion in the office. Some of us liked the basic idea of taking a book that is referred to in fiction (in this case, Christopher Isherwood's *Mister Norris Changes Trains*) but which did not previously exist. However, we all had grave reservations about the length of some of your sentences: although Joyce used the device to good effect in *Ulysses* for Molly Bloom's soliloquy, the absence of conventional punctuation from the whole of Chapter 9 – 150 MS pages – would test the stamina of even the most dedicated reader.

Although the book is not without merit and a sort of feral power, I regret that it does not quite fit into either our existing list or our programme of forthcoming publications.

I am sorry to disappoint you but wish you the best of luck with it elsewhere.

I return the manuscript herewith.

Yours in letters

Jacob Pursey

Editor in Chief

The valediction was Jake's – he thought it a nice touch – but the rest of this note and dozens like it were all the work of Ella

Bethune. She knew enough about literature to recognise references to other works; she'd not have fallen for the Salinger. She was polite and sensitive but firm and brooked no contradiction. She never made the elementary mistake of asking for changes and thus increasing the possibility that the works might be resubmitted. Neither did she say that she looked forward to the author's next effort: that was a ruse employed by some publishers and agents who hoped that in the year or two that it took him to knock out another couple of hundred thousand words he might have died. An unequivocal no was the only language these people understood, and particularly crucial in the case of this Grylls, who mentioned in his covering letter that Montague Dawson was not the only fictional author whose unwritten work he had committed to paper. The other imaginary book he had completed was *Dogs Have No Uncles* by F.X. Trapnel, which Anthony Powell had invented but unaccountably failed to write. Grylls would be only too pleased to submit it if VI looked favourably on *The Private Diary*. He also claimed to be making significant progress with another work, *The Furrow* by Stephen Johnson, a character in Radclyffe Hall.

§

"George Mascaret?"

"Hey, I know that voice. Good to hear you; how's every damn thing?"

Bugger, thought George. I always say that whenever he calls. And I'm trying to come across as sparky and creative and original. He'll think I'm a complete dork.

"Mustn't grumble", said Jez Yaxley, thinking Jesus I always say that to him. But then as he always says the same thing to me he leaves me no option. What a total knob.

"About your *101 Reasons* thing. It's good, we like it but…"

"Aaah, but."

"Yes, but, but just hold on. Although it's really not for us, we have got another project that we think might be right up your passage."

Chapter Four: Passing Sentences

Roosevelt's Secret Agent: The Plot to Kill Quisling by Jan Hoffmann, Codename "Jig How". Ella Bethune was braced for disappointment when she opened it. She said she'd learned that talking a good book is not the same as writing it, and that the two activities are often mutually exclusive. But that was no more than a prejudice; she'd thought it since before she went to university and, never having reviewed her position, pressganged her subsequent experiences into service of the theory.

The author lacked confidence: she glossed things that required no explanation and assumed knowledge that was most likely the preserve of spies and soldiers. Her prose was tabloid journalese, characterised by excessive fondness for the staccato verb. Yet her story was irresistible, a tale of courage in the face of extreme jeopardy: the assassination attempt itself and the flight from the Nasjonal Samling into the mountains around Geilo. Ella read it twice in an evening. The next morning she handed it to Jacob Pursey, tactfully directing his attention to the controversial bit in which the author claimed that the U.S. President had encouraged Klaus Fuchs and the Rosenbergs to pass nuclear secrets to the Soviet Union because he believed in maintaining the balance of global power.

Having thus had his card marked, Pursey didn't open the typescript; he scribbled "Worth a look?" on a scrap of paper, stapled it to the cover of the work and passed it to Baxter Stratton. Stratton didn't read it either – with Pursey's imprimatur, he was covered in the event of mishap – he merely gave it to Gill Furneaux. She stared into it as a clairvoyant fairground gypsy might contemplate a crystal ball. As the orb unmisted she foresaw fast bucks swirling in clouds eastwards over the Atlantic. She had the book couriered to Schloss Volkmer, where the chairman took a particular shine to the facsimile Hoffmann had supplied of a handwritten note:

Warm Springs

Georgia

April 1945

Jan Hoffmann (J.H.) was a member of my Nordic Action Group. She renounced her identity in the service of her country.

Jig How was one of the chosen few who knew that patriotism alone was not enough. Although her mission was thwarted, her brave deeds will forever be memorialized.

Sincerely

FDR

Max summoned his driver and made a special journey in to the office to tell Gill that she must get the book at any cost (within reason) and publish it with as much dispatch as possible (without losing sight of the normal boundaries of commercial prudence). He knew that interest in the story would have no time limit; they were both concerned about making up revenue lost to the Cardiff fraudster and the recent payment to Clarissa Newnham.

"Yesterday might not be too soon", he added in the special voice that he reserved for exhortation. Though meant to be winsome, this was widely interpreted as minatory.

Shortly thereafter Jan Hoffmann received a formal offer from Volkmer & Iles. Both the advance and the royalty were every bit as exiguous as a publisher might be expected to propose in a case where the author had no agent and had admitted that her sole objective was to see the work in print.

Among the senior executives who were not consulted about this publishing sensation was Willie Lechler but he, determined not to be ox-bowed out of the creative flow, filched a copy of the typescript and sent it to Herbert Hirsch, professor of governance and policy at the University of Alabama and author of VI's *Revisionist Readings in the New Deal*.

§

Not entirely for nothing had Jez Yaxley used the term "right up your passage". The work he commissioned from George Mascaret was a his-and-hers joke book.

Humour titles – books purporting to be funny – are as natural in autumn as falling leaves. What would make this publication different and, it was hoped, take the Christmas gift market by storm, was the format: two interlocking but detachable halves, with the spear side in the shape of a penis and two testicles and the distaff side in that of a female abdomen.

George was certain that if he had ever been about to propose such a work to any publisher he'd have gone to the meeting wearing a padded rubber suit in confident anticipation of being kicked down the stairs. He said he had to admit that he'd never done anything like this before. Jez said he didn't think that would be a problem; evidently concerned about what such a book might do to his own reputation (he was naturally less bothered about that of the author), he added that it wasn't his idea, he was merely the conduit, the facilitator, the poor sod with whom this particular buck was stopping.

"If I could invent stuff like this I'd be writing scripts in Hollywood."

Notwithstanding that George was unable to say, "I guess that's what I do", he accepted the commission. He then reported to Vivienne that he had been hired to write a book with, as he put it, "A prick on the verso and a clit on the erecto". She told him she didn't know what he was talking about so he drew it for her. They then tried together to work out which great aphorism was more appropriate: the Preacher's that there is no new thing under the sun or Juvenal's that it is difficult not to write satire.

§

Colin Dodd started off thinking that his new job was a doss – a bit more money, a lot less work. It came with a pleasing title that struck awe into the hearts of all but his most recalcitrantly malcontent friends and disaffected colleagues. But after three months he found that the systems he tried to impose, unambitious though they were – checklists and neat piles of papers – were first subverted and then overwhelmed by the inchoate mess that made Skidmore the house it was. Chaos out of order, the antithesis of literature.

He was sanguine about this, partly because, having recently completed his trial period and been confirmed in post, he was about as safe as it's possible to be, and partly because there was no one around to make his life a misery in the way that Jacob Pursey had managed so effortlessly.

Or so he thought until the endomorph befriended him. There were early indications that this smelly slob was never going to be Colin's dish. One came in the form of a disparaging comment about the number of authors who were poofs. Another was his generic term for the junior editors – "bottom-feeders" – which was used in contradistinction to "people like us". In meetings the endomorph took to prefacing remarks with "I know Colin thinks…" and appending to others the coda "I'm sure Colin will agree".

Through his failure to react to these presumptions, Colin Dodd communicated weakness. As some carnivores are reputed to detect the smell of fear and head straight to its source, it was not long before Marcus the publisher was on his case.

"Colin, there's a feeling you're taking too long over these."

"Too long" was seldom more than a working week of twelve-hour days; "these" were manuscripts, each of around fifty thousand words.

Colin, keen to appear to his new master in the image of a can-do kind of an editorial director, thereafter spent less time on the text and more on budgeting and scheduling. And so far from being thanked for his obedience, he got it in the neck from the endomorph for devoting insufficient attention to the holy writ.

"I found several literals in this, Colin. Is there something you need to discuss with me, perhaps a problem at home?" And then the snide coda, "Girlfriend trouble?", followed by a leer that seemed to invite Colin to enter a conspiracy of which he was the victim.

§

Most of the preparations for Quisling were standard procedure, but because the book was scheduled for publication before the next sales conference, VI recorded a telephone interview with Jan Hoffmann and copied it on to cassettes which were sent with the jacket and the advanced information sheets to all the reps and agents. Ella was busy with this by day and with piles of scripts in the evenings. She hoped for an epiphany but most of her nights were starless until, in among the autobiographical novels with no plot; the erotic works that demonstrated zero insight into human psychology and often a disturbing lack of awareness of the physically feasible; the children's stories that were unoriginal even if the reader failed to recognise the sources; and the memoirs that purported to be about how the authors were abused as children but which read like uneasy mixtures of psychobabble and score-settling... in among all these and more, she came upon the Mascaret.

Whether the writing was any good Ella found it hard to tell – her eyes had become so accustomed to the dark that any point of light was blinding – but the subject appealed to her and the work could at least be read and understood in a single pass:

"Women characteristically regard Formula One Grands Prix as processions of boy racers in phallic vehicles with holes drilled in their exhaust pipes; they regard team games as little more than a front for the players' real preoccupation, which is to get in the showers with their team mates.

"These attitudes may be neither informed nor completely enlightened, but at least among singles they can be in plain view. Couples, however, are under both self-generated and external pressure to moderate their hostility or at least to keep it under wraps. Is it not sad to see women who have cheated golf widowhood by caddying for their partners or even taking up the game themselves? Is it anything less than nauseating to hear a man on the way out of *Love Story* tell his wife that he thought it had its points and was quite effective?"

Contentious, parts of it, but you don't need to say nothing just because it's difficult to say something that is agreed. And a bit writerly, but at least the author was in some kind of a relationship with the English language, which was more than could be said for most of those who submitted their work for consideration. And it was complete, which was always a plus. Ella was amazed by the number of people who sent in the first two or three chapters with a promise to finish the book if the publisher liked the sample. Or an assurance that the rest of it could be forwarded immediately on request. Ella had decided that she could tell reliably from internal evidence – in works of fiction, openings that contained too few set-ups – that either this was a lie or that the complete work would be going nowhere other than straight back to the author. What was obvious to her – that any creation has to spring fully formed and as it were breathing into the world – had evidently not occurred to most of the hopefuls. Never show an unfinished article to a fool: the intervention of criticism into a work in progress would more or less guarantee that it never got completed.

Yet re the Mascaret doubt persisted. She was not sure why, and her first thought was that it was not really a VI book. But that couldn't be right, because even the most superficial perusal of Jake's now legendary complete list would demonstrate conclusively that they published pretty much anything that took their fancy. Perhaps she didn't want to propose it to Jake for fear that he would think she was trying to tell him something.

Unable to see what she could do with *101 Reasons for*

Staying Single, but reluctant to reject it, she put the typescript into her pending tray. There it gathered dust for three months.

§

Meanwhile George had much else to occupy him. He bought a dozen joke books as reminders of classics he'd heard but could seldom bring to mind. He watched a lot more telly than usual: he became a connoisseur of *Morecambe and Wise* and *The Two Ronnies*. He listened to BBC Radio Four every evening between six-thirty and seven. He got dispirited. The first joke he adapted ended up on paper in the following form:

"On their wedding night at a hotel in an exotic location, the happy couple are just getting ready for bed when the bride makes an audible gas emission.

"The groom hugs and kisses her and says: 'Did daddy's little baby make oof-poof with her botty-wotty?'

"Twenty-five years later, the pair return to the hotel in the exotic location in a bid to recapture past pleasures.

"As they are getting ready for bed, the wife again makes an audible gas emission.

"The husband carries on folding his socks and says: 'That's right, stink the fucking place out'."

It is, George told himself again, the arrangement of the material that is new.

§

Marcus the publisher and the endomorph stared into their coffee mugs. Their wistful looks concealed a smouldering republicanism engendered by the Duchess of York's decision not to sign their contract and to take her services elsewhere.

"Bitch."

"Pseudo-aristocratic tart."

"Ginger hoo-er."

"Oliver Cromwell was right."

"We've a hole in the schedule the size of that crater in Siberia."

"What crater in Siberia?"

"You know, the one where the meteor hit."

"Do you mean Tunguska?"

"Isn't that part of the Great Rift Valley?"

"I don't bloody know, do I? The question is, with what shall we fill it, dear chummy, dear chummy?"

§

George Mascaret had little difficulty with men's jokes about women, a rich but overworked seam. At first they were broadly divisible into three categories.

Category one, the puerile, a heading applicable even (or perhaps especially) to jokes involving old men:

"Two ninety-year-olds in the Athenaeum. First ninety-year-old says: 'I had an erection last week'.

"Second ninety-year-old replies: 'Well done, old boy! Bet

the wife was pleased'.

"First ninety-year-old says: 'Wife be damned. I managed to grab a taxi and nurse it down to Soho'."

Category two, the familiar, or at least those he reckoned most people would already know in outline if not in detail, which he drew himself:

"On a visit to the souk in Damascus, a man buys an ornamental jar. When he gets it back to his hotel room he removes the lid and out pops a genie who, suitably grateful, grants his liberator one wish. The man, an observant traveller, says that what he'd like most in the world is peace in the Middle East.

"The genie folds his arms and says: 'You know that's a complex problem; more powerful beings than I have tried and failed here; I'm a genie, not a miracle worker. Is there anything else you'd like?'

"The man thinks for a moment and then replies: 'Well on a personal level, I'd really like it if my wife could be persuaded to give me a blow job'.

"The genie scratches his chin: 'When you say "peace", what exactly do you mean?'"

Category three, jokes that were both puerile and familiar, but which had to be included to make the work comprehensive. These he wrote down without embellishment:

"She was only the fisherman's daughter but when she saw his rod she reeled."

As he delved, he unearthed a fourth category, one-liners

that might get a laugh in the hands of a comedian but which were sardonic commentaries rather than jokes in any normally accepted sense of the term. These had to be included if he was to have any hope of making the required length:

"Before I married I had no one to finish my sentences for me".

Women's jokes about men were a harder assignment. There was less material and what there was wasn't much cop. He discerned no trends or patterns; faute de mieux he had to use pretty well all the material he found. To apply his own stamp, he related some of it in the form of extracts from an imaginary phrasebook:

"Manspeak: 'Can I give you a hand, darling?'

"English: 'Where's my dinner, bitch?'"

Also conscripted was a platoon of similes; these included:

"Men are like… parking places. All the good ones are taken…

"… photocopiers. You need them for reproduction, but that's about it…

"… lava lamps. Fun to look at, but not very bright…".

As the going got tough, George consoled himself with the thought that books that are easy to write are hard to read. When he started to think, not for the first time, "For this you went to Oxford?", he screwed his determination to the typewriter keyboard by reminding himself of greater sacrifices made by other authors. Samuel Johnson wrote *Rasselas* to fund the care of his sick mother; by the time he got paid he had to spend the money on her funeral. The only way that John Kennedy Toole could get his books in print was by topping himself.

§

A prosperous publisher would have responded to the need for what the endomorph called "more product asap" by either buying in the work of established authors or coming up with new concepts. But Skidmore was too indigent to afford first-class stamps – the Duchess's advance would have come from a bank loan – and the few members of staff who stood even a chance of recognising an idea if it disrobed in front of them were too despondent to raise a gallop about anything. The sole exception was newbie Colin Dodd who, still anxious to oblige, now hit the slush pile like a speeding snowplough. Yet though the waters thus disturbed sprayed upwards and outwards in a high and productive-looking V they gave up nothing of merit: the unsolicited submissions on his desk were no better than those on that of any other editor in town.

A month later, the endomorph told him in confidence that Marcus the p was under great strain because unless something turned up PDQ there would have to be sacrifices and he really hated taking the bread out of people's mouths, especially in the run-up to Christmas. And Colin knew exactly what this meant: it meant greater love than this hath no employer, to give up his staff to save his own neck. He was also aware of another fact of corporate life: last in, first out.

§

"Hi there, George, thanks for the stuff, it looks pretty good on the whole but I've got a couple of queries if we could just go through them now."

Jez Yaxley rushed all this out in one breath to avoid the usual exordium about hanging and not grumbling. It put George in mind of Ratty reciting picnic ingredients in *The Wind in the Willows*.

"coldtonguecoldhamcoldbeefpickledgherkins…".

"Page twenty-three, the one about football I just don't get."

"Aah."

"Maybe if you could explain it to me…"

"If you don't like it, I can take it out."

"No, no, it's not that, it's simply that I don't…"

"If a joke needs explaining, it isn't a joke."

"Sometimes that's true, but just indulge me, will you?"

"Okay. She was only the football manager's daughter but she didn't half like her Huddersfield – that is, udders as in cow's teats and feeled as in the past participle of feel – and her Arsenal, which is 'and her arse and all', as in in addition, yes?"

"Aah yes, now I get it."

"It's an old music hall gag. It works if you say it in a northern accent."

"Do you think we should flag that?"

"I don't see how."

"Maybe start with 'A Yorkshireman said'?"

"Isn't that too much of a dig in the ribs?"

"Or write it in the dialect?"

"But then how do you show that you're using the names of the clubs?"

"Maybe you're right; best take it out."

§

"Much of it was foreseeable but I thought I could handle it because I was in a better position on a slightly higher rung. Mainly though, as it turns out, the place is just like VI: authors who should no more be let loose with a Biro than Herod should be hired as a babysitter; absurd arguments about the correct position of the colon, which is up the arse; the constant feeling that no book is ever completed, it's only abandoned; trolley-dollies in marketing and publicity who think their jobs will get them into a clinch with Piers Paul Read and or Paul Theroux; senior managers who are so useless that I sometimes think if they got hired I must be in with a fighting chance of getting picked for the British Olympic relay team."

Thus Colin Dodd in a Soho pub to Tim Etchells, the one known as Eenie, who then told him:

"If it's any consolation, you got out at just the right time. The CAUC has become so important that he no longer has time to look over your shoulder, but now you have to kiss his ring every week at progress meetings, a misnomer if ever there was one because you spend so long in them that you never get round to actually doing anything."

Colin didn't want to hear about his former place of work: no wife of Lot, he. So what both men would recall as a conversation proceeded for a while along the parallel lines of two monologues. Colin continued:

"The big difference at Skidmore is the unashamed lack of reconstruction. No minority is safe – blacks, Jews, lefties, homosexuals of course. On the rare occasions they have a drinks' party – there's no money – they go around saying 'Ooh I can't possibly touch his glass, I might get AIDS'. And that attitude informs their dealings with everyone. They say they wouldn't have signed Bruce Chatwin – as if that would ever have been a possibility – because he dropped his anchor in a foreign port."

Eenie, seeing that accounts of his own experiences and views were not on tonight's agenda, acceded to the inevitable and asked Colin some more about Colin:

"Why don't you tell them you're straight?"

He'd always wondered, not just about why he never said.

"They've made up their minds and thoughts are so rare and precious to them that if they ever have one they hang onto it like a Staffordshire bull terrier hangs on to the postman's goolies. Besides, I don't want to be in their club."

"Does it worry you that people think you're gay?"

"It used to, but then for reasons I don't fully understand – maturity, atrophy, who knows? – I stopped caring. There's a select coterie that knows the truth and that'll do for me. Anyway, I can't go around saying 'Hey, I'm so het' because they'd all just think the lady doth protest too much. And maybe the uncertainty makes me more interesting to women. Or at least less boring."

These thoughts of the past finally reminded Colin of his time at Volkmer & Iles. There had been a woman there in whom he'd been vaguely interested, but they'd never even got so far as a date.

"How's Ella, by the way?"

Tim wondered if Colin had dropped this name to lay a false trail, but in the same instant decided that this was just another of those questions that would abide for eternity.

"You're so asking the wrong person. I feel I understand her less than almost anyone I've ever met. She's intelligent, sensitive, gentle, cultivated, attractive..."

At the last epithet Colin made a face and wobbled a flat hand. Tim thought that the lady might have mentioned protesting too much because that was exactly what she was doing. But his response betrayed no such suspicion.

"Just because she doesn't come on to anyone."

"Aah, but we both know that's not entirely true."

"Quite so, and that's at the heart of the mystery. What could she ever have seen in Jacob Pursey?"

"How ever low a woman sinks she'll always find a man who's sunk lower."

"Nietzsche?"

"No, a Dodd original."

"Anyway, she's paying for her indiscretion now."

§

If people were competitive in pursuit of an identifiable prize that only one of them could win, it might be possible to understand and even perhaps to sympathise with their desire to neutralise or eliminate the opposition. But when all they can hope to achieve through their machinations is the avoidance of blame, and by it to extend their half-lives in work, their ambitions seem pitiable.

That was the view of the chief buyer at W.H. Smith, who asked Jake how come he was both sales manager and editor in chief.

"You must admit that's an unusual combination, even in book publishing."

Ignoring the faintly insulting way in which he managed to make the latter title sound as if it were in inverted commas, Pursey replied:

"I knew what I wanted and I went for it."

But neither part of that statement was true. Pursey had no vocation and his miraculous rise had been largely fortuitous. He did, however, have razor-sharp elbows, and at the next editorial plenum they set about striping the lettuce leaf.

"So one in every four of your titles is running late."

"I think you'll find that's about par for the course", said Willie Lechler. "Working with academics is like herding cats."

"I notice that one of them is more than a year behind schedule." Pursey said the last word the American way.

"That's probably the Jinnah biography, you know, the one that doesn't exist. We got so many orders for it that it started appearing on the printouts."

Jake rolled down his sleeves to sheathe his most potent weapons.

"At least the Spanish and Portuguese Philologias are coming, finally."

"Yes, Jake, you'll find they were well worth waiting for."

Gill Furneaux didn't like embarrassment unless she was causing it so she moved to the next agenda item, general books, and asked her sales manager to report.

"The Cree memoirs: copies are due in the warehouse next Thursday. We've subscribed just over a thousand in the UK; not much in export, but we weren't expecting anything. The big one, though, is *Roosevelt's Secret Agent*. I think some – all? – of you have read it…."

Willie was among those who nodded, but if Pursey noticed he could not have known the true significance of the gesture and would probably have thought that the editorial director was just being a creep.

"There's every reason to believe that this is the non-fiction hit of the year. We've sold U.S. rights, a Norwegian edition of course and we're talking to three Sunday newspapers about serialisation."

Then Gill said: "In view of all those books that disappeared up Cwm Rhondda, we need more turnover fast. Is there anything we can rush out?"

No response.

"What about the slush pile?"

"I think Ella is the person best placed to talk to this."

This assertion made Willie bilious, not just because of the abominable phraseology. He was revolted by the ease with which Pursey passed the buck and excruciated by the thought that no one else seemed to notice or care.

"I gather you've not been having a lot of luck", said Baxter.

"That's not entirely true."

"I was thinking of *The Catcher in the Rye.*"

Afraid of how Ella might respond to this, Pursey put in:

"Let's not worry about that, no one died; carry on."

"Pretty well all the novels I get are non-starters", Ella continued.

"So is there any benefit in what you're doing editorially?" asked Gill.

"Of course there is", said Baxter. "Even if it's only waste disposal, the bins still need emptying. Dear John letters have to be sent."

"Indeed they do", Gill said pointedly to Baxter, then soothingly to Ella: "Sorry, I'm paid to ask awkward questions. Have you got anything that we could just bang out, humour or general interest?"

"Well there are numerous non-fiction things. Someone just sent in an Essex Girl Joke Book."

Gill pulled a face which emboldened Baxter to say: "Yawnarama".

"It's all right if you like books of jokes about girls from Essex."

"It's been done before."

"They're all just recycled blonde jokes, aren't they?"

"Old wine in new bottles."

"Book-making at its worst."

"Anyway", said Gill, "I'm saying no to that. But we need five popular titles that we can shift in till-mounted packs of ten". Then the rhetorical coda: "Does that seem possible?" She took no reply as a yes.

§

The endomorph pointed Colin Dodd in the direction of a pile of manuscripts that looked as if they had been untouched since Wynkyn de Worde first moved metal type.

"These are all works to which we own the rights but which we haven't published because we thought we had bigger fish to fry. Maybe you can find something worthwhile."

He made this sound like an act of kindness but it was motivated by self-interest: although his buck-passing proficiency was dependable enough to make him confident that the axe would fall on Colin's head before his own, he was not so sure that, once the blood bath started running, he would not be expected to make his own contribution to its inflow.

"You might need to kick them around a bit. You know, update some of the references, make minor improvements as you see fit. You can even spend a bit on line drawings if you want to, as long as you're careful. Basically, anything there that you think might work, just use it. Marcus and I will rely on your judgment."

So after years of being chained to a perch, Colin was suddenly cleared to go soaring. Like a hawk. But also like Icarus. And look what happened to him. But then again one hour of glorious life beats an age without a name, and all that. What was the worst that could happen? He'd get the boot. But so? What went for his previous employer – the oft-quoted maxim that getting sacked by Volkmer & Iles was like getting frogmarched out of a leper colony – was true in spades of Skidmore.

§

"Let muffled bells ring out," said George Mascaret, brandishing a letter. "We have a taker for the marriage book. The 'editor in chief', no less, of Volkmer & Iles, publisher of, inter alios, Clarissa Newnham."

"Does this mean I don't have to go in today?" said Vivienne, who was just about to leave for work.

"Not unless you think we can survive on a two-thousand advance against a five per cent royalty."

"Perhaps hold on till you hear back from the Americans?"

"If I wait that long it'll probably be part of my estate; time has no meaning for these people."

"Still, it's something. When did you last have one of your ideas accepted?"

"Probably when I proposed to you. But this wasn't strictly a Mascaret original, remember, it was Skidmark's."

"Well it's yours now", said Vivienne. "You'll have to do the children's tea; I'll cook for us when I get home. And oh", she added as she closed the door behind her, "bravissimo".

§

Dear Willie Lechler

Since I do not know you personally I am unable to judge whether the contents of your package were intended as a joke. In that case, it is not a very funny one. If, as I fear, they are supposed to be taken seriously, I scarcely know where to begin.

My suspicions were aroused by the very idea that Roosevelt cared or felt he could do anything about the occupation of Norway. They intensified on reaching the first of the reported conversations between the author and the President, all of which are completely incredible.

What clinched it was the letter. Ignoring the likelihood that by April 1945 FDR would have been in no physical condition to give dictation, let alone to write himself, even the most cursory examination of the authenticated correspondence would show beyond a peradventure that this is not Roosevelt's handwriting.

I cannot adequately express my dismay at the realization that a reputable house such as Volkmer & Iles, publisher of distinguished academic work and some high-grade fiction, should contemplate, even for a moment, commissioning a work so patently bogus. I will not humiliate you or the author (some kind of performance artist? A delusional schizophrenic?) by bringing this obvious scam to public attention; however in the light of it I may have to think more than once about where to place my own future work.

Sincerely

Herb Hirsch

P.S. Since drafting this, I ran the passage about Ms Hoffmann's arrival in Norway past a colleague, a keen aeronaut. I trust this does not count as a breach of confidence (trick). He said the idea that you could drop from a low-flying Westland Lysander and land uninjured stretches credibility way beyond breaking point. The plane could not have been less than twenty feet above the ground and would not have been travelling at less than 45 m.p.h. I rest my (parachute) case.

HH

§

Occasionally it happens when you read a book or hear a piece of music for the first time that you feel you already know it. Not in the old hat way or the plagiarist way, but in the way that combines the shock of the new with the comfort of the womb. (Not that the womb is necessarily all it's cracked up to be: if it were that great we might not struggle so much to get out of it. But it's the conventional byword for anywhere safe and warm, so stet.) A brand new work that goes straight from the stocks to the pantheon, with none of the marketing or word-of-mouth reputation-building that normally comes in between. Well that was the feeling Marcus the publisher got when the endomorph presented him with *Advice to Persons About to Marry*. He liked everything about it: the title, taken by Colin Dodd from a famous article in *Punch*; the jacket, commissioned by the same, featuring a cartoon of Prince Charles and Princess Diana looking soulfully in opposite directions; and above all the text, much of which had the assurance of a master. He was particularly taken with the conceit about a new version of *The Sound of Music* in which the von Trapps fall in a spray of bullets. He felt he'd known it all his life.

But Marcus the publisher wasn't a fool. He'd read somewhere that the number of one's brain cells diminishes in middle age, and he'd made errors of judgment before that he'd probably got away with only because he owned the company and there was consequently no one to sack him.

"Can you recall how we came by this book in the first place?"

"It was one of Robin's eggs", said the endomorph.

This had become Skidmore code for crap.

"But on a second look, it's probably all right, isn't it? In fact, I think it's really got something. Why didn't we go ahead with it the first time? Was the author a cunt?"

"Probably. But Colin doesn't have a note of who wrote it."

"It was before my time", Colin protested limply.

Marcus responded with a look that might have said, What else can you expect in a place like this? but could equally have been taken as What kind of an excuse do you call that?

§

The Hirsch letter conferred power on Willie Lechler but he was uncertain how to exercise it. He could use it to demonstrate the foolhardiness of leaving editorial decisions in the hands of sales and marketing, a move that might enable him to reclaim all his pre-Pursey responsibilities. But he was compromised by the manner in which he had acquired the Hoffmann typescript. Looking back, he would reflect that he should have gone straight to Max Volkmer. Timidity stayed his hand: he'd always thought that top executives paid other people to get things done and didn't want to hear about their internecine rivalries.

However, he was smart enough to bypass the CAUC and the Toothy Rapist. He came in early one morning and left the letter on the desk of the managing director. When Gill Furneaux finished reading it she felt Old Testamental, and foresaw imminent leaving parties for Baxter and Jake. She rang the production controller and instructed him to put the Hoffmann on hold. She then summoned Ella Bethune and told her what she wanted her to do.

§

After all the jokes that Jez Yaxley didn't understand had been removed and author and publisher had been unable to agree on replacements, Wilby Bestsellers increased the print size by two points and stuck in a couple of royalty-free agency photographs to make fifteen thousand words fill the space of the twenty thousand they had originally commissioned. If George Mascaret had written only the lower number, he'd have been getting half a pound per hundred words, rather than his usual fifteen pee. But he'd also had to produce all the material that was subsequently rejected. From the artistic perspective, the book looked like an impending disaster. George asked if he could use a pseudonym but Jez wasn't having it:

"Are you ashamed of what you've done? Are you suggesting that it's not your best work?"

"No, Jez, of course not."

§

A week after Ella Bethune's meeting with Gill Furneaux, this arrived by airmail from upstate New York:

Dear Ella

I have just received your letter and the returned MS.

I am very sad. I do not understand your reference to "discrepancies". I should like to know what they are.

While I appreciate your efforts to turn my memoirs into a book,

I feel that you have failed to convince your masters and mistresses of the secrecy that still surrounds my war, even after all this time.

As regards the missing details: you recall that in the book I mention my sister, who had to leave home. I did not go further into those sad events to spare everyone's feelings, even though she is now dead, but the truth is that she had a brain tumour which led her to do queer things. One of her worst acts was to destroy all my private papers, including official documents and letters that would have verified everything.

I note that you have not returned the copy of the letter that Professor Hirsch queried: will you please return it?

Please thank the directors for the advance. I will discuss this with my attorney and if he thinks I have a right to it I will put it into the research fund for a neutron beam gun which will be a cure for all terminal cancers.

Dear Ella, thank you so very much for all your efforts. I am sorry that it should end this way. All the very best in the future – you will go far.

Sincerely

Jan Hoffmann

§

The Denver shower never mentioned *101 Reasons*. Although that no longer mattered to George Mascaret, he did wonder if their latest proposal had been prompted by his submission or arrived merely by coincidence.

They offered him a commission to edit *Bad Language*, a book for university freshmen on rude words. An interesting subject, but not the way it was treated here. The rubric contained strict rules of engagement: what the publisher called "the f-word" could be used sparingly but "the c-word" and "the n-word" were absolutely forbidden; they could not even be alluded to. These were particularly exacting requirements given that almost every page of the book seemed to contain more effs, cees and ens than a latrine wall in a new town tenement.

Then George read the opening paragraph:

"Slang, in its ability to incite controversy, elicit emotion, provide comic relief and agitate sexual norms, speaks to tremendous power of language as it circulates in discursive space".

And that was as good as it got; the author popped his best shot first. Among the things that leapt off later pages to get George's goat was a sentence beginning: "In the view of one very serious commentator…". Setting aside the implication that there are three grades – commentators, serious commentators and very serious commentators – if George took the job he would have to ask the author to identify this great guru. And direct contact was a consummation devoutly to be avoided at all costs. And if the author bothered to respond, he would most likely not remember the source. And then the passage would have to be rewritten. And in the unlikely event that the author agreed to undertake this assignment, he would almost certainly fail to complete it before the deadline. And the likeliest outcome was that the whole book would end up being written by the editor.

The writer was so fond of rhetorical questions that they could not accurately be described as verbal mannerisms or tics; they were more like preclinical convulsions. He reached for them in moments of crisis, which were numerous and of which Mascaret identified two types. Type one, whenever he was in danger of revealing the threadbareness of his thoughts:

"Was it not Masters and Johnson who taught us that the human sexual response cycle has four stages?"

Yes, perhaps, if you tell us so. Then again, maybe it's ancient wisdom, a.k.a. common knowledge, here ascribed to famous authors in the hope of thus concealing its essential banality. Alternatively, "four stages" could be arbitrary compartmentalisation of a phenomenon that might be divided into as many parts as you fancied or needed for your argument.

Type two arose when the author wanted to associate his implausible hypotheses with the giants of psychoanalysis, who wouldn't be able to object to his blasphemy because they were all dead:

"What might Ferenczi have made of the ambivalence of *tart*, which one user might employ as the identifier of a comestible, but which might equally be taken by a listener or reader, in even context, to refer to a flirtatious or promiscuous woman?"

Tricky one, that: right up there with questions like "What would have happened if Othello had been dropped into Hamlet's situation? Would we have ended up with *Macbeth*?"

Skimming the rest of it, George Mascaret found several more obstacles. A nursery rhyme came to him in altered form:

"We're going on an edit,
It's going to have to be a big one;
We're not scared.
Uh-oh: screeds of dreck;
We can't make sense of them
We can't get round them
We can't kill the author (sadly)
We'll have to take a machete to them
Heigh-ho never mind
It'll all be the same in a hundred years".

He concluded that the work was as embarrassing as syphilis but harder to cure; life was too short and the fee too small. Full of optimism that he was moving on to a new phase of life, from writer-cum-editor to full-time author, he further decided that he no longer needed this drudgery. He wondered for a moment if this was wise – freelances are supposed never to say no to anything. He recalled Stevenson's view that men "court the strokes of destiny, and rush towards anything decisive, that it may free them from suspense though at the cost of ruin. It is one of the many minor forms of suicide". But still he turned it down.

§

The beauty of collective responsibility is that it lets everyone off the hook. Gill Furneaux, Baxter Stratton and Jacob Pursey were all in the clear over Quisling because they had followed correct procedure by passing the book up the chain of command. For a moment Willie Lechler was in the frame for disloyalty but he avoided retribution because the others knew they should not have omitted him from their original discussions. As the most junior member of the pack, Ella got an informal talking-to from Gill about the dangers of excessive enthusiasm. At first this struck her as rich, not to say fruity, given that the general level of zeal in the place was reminiscent of that attributed by Cat Stevens to the workforce at Matthew and Son. But the criticism was gently made over a two-hour lunch at Sheekey's, during which the M.D.'s main theme was that the final decision had been the chairman's, and like all great entrepreneurs he was a law unto himself: woman proposes but Max disposes.

§

George Mascaret's vestigial worries that he might have done the wrong thing by saying no to *Bad Language* were banished when he received in the post half a dozen presentation copies of his latest work. No doubt about it, VI produced a good-looking book. *101 Reasons for Staying Single* was a small hardback, seven and a half inches tall, four and three-quarter inches wide and an inch thick. On the jacket was a full-colour montage of four once-great couples – Henry VIII and Catherine of Aragon; Ronald Reagan and Jane Wyman; Princess Anne and Mark Phillips; Roger Vadim and Brigitte Bardot – each with a white lightning rip between them.

On the back flap he found a photograph of himself that he thought made him look a right wanker sat in his study in front of a shelf full of learned-looking books that he'd never read. Beneath it was the legend:

"George Mascaret is a prolific author under his own name and a host of pseudonyms. No recker of his own rede, he is happily married with three children".

He wasn't entirely pleased with this either. He now thought that "happily" was overegging the pudding. Not that he was unhappy, it was just that statements like that are devalued by people who make them mendaciously. He couldn't imagine life without Vivienne, but he couldn't go around saying that in case people took it as a coded expression of a desire to strangle her and stash her body beneath the floorboards.

Still, the description represented a small but significant victory: when he'd submitted it, Ella came back to him with the editor in chief's response that it was off-message and obscure. George affected not to know what she was driving at. Ella put it to him that, although she recognised the literary allusion, gentle readers might not. George, in unusually combative mood, asked her if she was aware of the FOFO principle of pedagogy. Before she had a chance to own that she did not, he explained that it was an acronym of "fuck off and find out", which is what he thought anyone who didn't know anything should always do.

Such intransigence would have got up the nose and back of many editors, but Ella was impressed by George's spirit and, in spite of the Hoffmann disaster, still had the self-assurance to let half-decent authors have most of what they wanted. She anticipated, correctly as it turned out, that the colleague who objected to it in unedited form would not notice it in the final version.

§

Some businesses have dress-down Fridays. Skidmore had no sartorial rules and marked the end of their week in a different way. The hebdomadal festivities began at one o'clock sharp.

"Marcus and I are going for a sesh at The Albion; do you want to join us?"

"I won't, thanks all the same; I want to push off early."

"I wouldn't worry about that; we'll be in till closing time."

"Unfortunately I've got to drive later. I'm going to stay with a friend in the country."

The endomorph conveyed Colin's refusal to Marcus the publisher: "He says he won't be taking wine with the officers today; he's going cottaging in Brighton."

§

"A present?" said George in not entirely mock excitement.

"I'm not sure you'll like it", Vivienne replied as she handed him a Hatchards bag.

George removed from it a copy of *Advice to Persons About to Marry*.

"Looks okay to me. Thank you very much."

"No, I mean it. I think you'll find some similarities to one-o-one."

"Competing product? Bring it on! The jacket's weak – Chas and Di, what a cliché! – it's all flippy-floppy, not like my handsomely cased volume; it costs a pound more and it doesn't have an author. Rubbish."

He glanced at the spine: "That's Skidmore for you."

"George, really, look inside; this may be serious."

And he looked and he saw and after much page-flipping he said: "The slags! The fucking slags! They haven't even changed the bastard words".

§

With the money he'd made from his Welsh venture, Ross Runnacles sent out invoices for arbitrary amounts of between fifty and one hundred pounds for unitemised "general services" to ten thousand addresses, businesses and private individuals, which he transcribed himself from London telephone directories. He received in return several queries, which he ignored, but netted a total of just over twenty thousand pounds from people who paid up without demur. He used the profit to finance his next project.

Chapter Five: The Walnut Principle

They do say that the lie is halfway round the block before the truth has got its boots on; they do seldom mention that bad news can outstrip the pair of them.

The third person to notice that the contents of *101 Reasons for Staying Single* were the same as those of *Advice to Persons About to Marry* was a shop assistant who made the discovery while unpacking a box of each title in the stock room at W.H. Smith Brent Cross. She rang head office in Swindon, ostensibly to seek advice but really to share the joke.

After visiting the central warehouse and there confirming that his informant was not mistaken, the chief buyer decided that the lickspittle running dogs of British publishing needed their noses rubbing in the mess they'd made. Since he could make only one call at a time, he bypassed Skidmore, to the name of whose sales manager he was unable put a face and who therefore could never have offended him, and got straight on to Volkmer & Iles, of whose ditto the same could not be said. Such was his excitement at the prospect that he never checked the time. If he had he'd probably not have bothered dialling, because he knew that nine o'clock was too early for an executive of Jacob Pursey's eminence to be at his workstation. He left a message with the switchboard operator but ringing back wasn't in the CAUC's job description – he was too busy and important to waste time on clients unless he was selling them something. So, without much else that needed doing urgently that morning, the chief buyer kept trying. He eventually got through at a quarter to eleven.

"Listen to this."

He read out a short paragraph, then gave the title of the work from which it came. To ensure that Jake knew what was being referred to, he added that it was a Volkmer & Iles book, one of their latest publications.

"Now, for the purpose of comparison, hear this."

He then quoted an identical passage from the Skidmore paperback. Hearing Pursey flounder, he threw in another example to heighten the effect.

"Notice any similarities? That's how they are all the way through: exactly the same in every detail apart from the title, the binding, the ISBN, the layout and possibly the typeface."

"Those are themselves significant differences."

This was lame, and Pursey's voice revealed that he knew it.

"But not as significant as the words on the page, which are normally what makes a book different from any other."

Pursey rallied with a stronger riposte:

"Clearly Skidmore have plagiarised our text."

"But their book was published two weeks before yours."

"Pub dates mean nothing."

Neither party was convinced. Pursey said he'd look into it. He spent the next three hours in crisis meetings.

§

George Mascaret decided against ringing Skidmore because he had no idea what he'd say or how they might respond. Contacting Volkmer & Iles was out of the question: none of this was their fault. While he was still deliberating – an open-ended assignment that might have postponed action to beyond the last syllable of recorded time – the phone rang. It was Ella Bethune. She told him what had happened and his silence made her think, contrary to her expectations, that it was all a complete surprise to him, an impression he did nothing to dispel.

"We need to meet."

"Yes, that's right, I think we should. Let me just find my diary."

"By close of business today."

"I'm not too sure about that. I need to pick up my children from school...."

"Tomorrow morning then."

"That's probably okay. There's a ten-o-nine via Haywards Heath that gets in to Victoria at eleven twenty-two."

Ella's response chilled his ear.

"Ten o'clock sharp at our offices, without fail, please."

"This is all a bit precipitate, isn't it?"

"Ask at reception for Max Volkmer."

§

When a two-man delegation from VI pitched up unannounced at Skidmore, Marcus the publisher thought it must be one of those commercial raiding parties he'd heard about, and wondered if this was how takeover bids usually began.

As the marauders were swished out of the glitzy reception area and into the damp dump at the back, the seedier of them lifted a copy of *Advice to Persons About to Marry* from the display of new titles. Once they'd been installed in the multipurpose fish tank that served as meeting room and script depository, this book became Exhibit A; Exhibit B was the copy they'd brought with them of *101 Reasons*.

The less repugnant-looking boarder was Willie Lechler. Marcus the publisher had come across him before at book fairs and literary festivals and the two of them sometimes talked on the phone, most recently when Willie had tried to palm off the Cree memoirs. Marcus wasn't having any of them – too much agg, too little return – and it hadn't taken the two men long to agree that the work was a non-starter. Its appearance shortly afterwards near the top of the VI new books list led Marcus to the conclusion that Willie, in spite of his highfalutin job title, was a powerless functionary, the worst kind of publishing hack. This prejudice had been reinforced by the article in *Private Eye*. But in his current aspect Willie Lechler came over like a zealot who's just received a testimonial signed by God in all three persons. No vegetable he now, unless it was the world's first carnivorous lettuce.

He outlined the facts more trenchantly than he should by

rights have been able to, given that the case was without precedent and that everything he knew about it he had gleaned from Jacob Pursey, whom he trusted no further than he could fling a Routemaster and who no longer explained anything to anyone: in his bad eminence the CAUC now communicated almost exclusively in imperatives, like an editorial in the *Daily Express*.

At first Marcus the publisher boggled so much that he feared his responses might appear unconvincing. Quickly, though, he formulated his own view of the matter. He dismissed as ludicrous Willie's suggestion that Skidmore had by some unaccounted method purloined the VI book and given it a different title in a pitiful attempt to conceal its true identity.

"I can tell you exactly what's happened."

Willie made the floor-is-yours gesture.

"The fucking author's fucking sold it fucking twice."

Willie's companion, who had not introduced himself and thus far played the role of the wise monkey that takes it all in and says nothing, now mirthlessly flashed a load of top incisors that looked like a row of dishwashers on display in a department store.

"That's what we thought. Obviously the writer's at the head of the queue for the mother of all kickings. However, we don't think we'll get much change out of him because he won't have any."

"Any what?" said Marcus, the thread momentarily slipping from his grasp.

"Change. You know, wonga. Dosh. The stuff we're all after. Munee."

He illustrated this by rubbing his thumb and forefinger together.

Seeing the glimmer of an opportunity to get onside with his assailants and perhaps even to unite with them against a common enemy, Marcus the p said:

"No, indeed, but the least we can do is make sure he never works again. Ruin him. I'm well up for that."

The VI men looked at each other to decide which of them would deliver what in rehearsal they had foreseen as the coup de grâce. Willie left it with the white goods department.

"Certainly we can join forces in a concerted effort to achieve that most desirable of resolutions. In the meantime, may we assume that you will immediately withdraw your title and pulp it?"

If Marcus looked green it was mould not inexperience.

"As long as I may take it that you will also withdraw and pulp yours."

Willie took from his briefcase a copy of Exhibit C, a contract signed by Ella Bethune for Volkmer & Iles and by George Louis Mascaret on his own account.

"Our position is that we are the original publishers of this work."

Marcus the publisher ran his eyes over the document and jabbed his index finger on the date.

"I think you'll find we owned the rights way before then."

"If that indeed turns out to be the case, we may have a different problem. Not that we doubt your word, of course, it's merely that you would have to let us have sight of documentation in support of that claim."

"We're having some refurbishments, everything's a bit what I like to call piggledy-higgledy at the moment, but we'll certainly dig out our copy of the author agreement and get it over to you in the next day or so. Okay? Then we can take it from there."

Willie got a strong sense that Marcus was lying, not just about the internal facelift, but he gave him twenty-four hours to marshal his defence.

Realising that this was about as good as it was going to get, the p relaxed a little.

"The whole thing is most regrettable. Authors, eh, who'd have 'em? Now, gentlemen, I'd love to spend longer with you but if there's nothing else you really must excuse me, I've got a conference call booked with Funk & Wagnalls."

As the VI men reached the exit, the one with the mouth full of monumental masonry delivered a parting shot in the hushed tones adopted by TV soap opera villains when they're trying to come over hard and threatening:

"I do hope we can sort this amicably, without having to get all lawyered up. That would be most unpleasant."

Marcus made like that was the nicest thing anyone had ever said to him. Shaking the asshole's hand, he replied:

"We'll be in touch very soon. Thanks so much for dropping

by. Great to meet you. Lovely to see you again, Willie. Take care."

§

"Let me see if I've got this right", said the solicitor. "You were approached by a publisher who paid you an advance to write a book. You completed the work and submitted it – 'filed your copy'…"

He liked to use his clients' business argot whenever possible; it gave him a kick and, he thought, reassured them that he was à la page. The phrase felt so good on his tongue that he said it again.

"That's right, isn't it, filed your copy on or before the due date. The publisher subsequently decided not to go ahead, for reasons that you were never officially told, but there was no suggestion at any time that you'd broken the agreement. Do you have a contract?"

"No, but I have an invoice and proof of payment."

"They may amount to the same thing. And then you placed the work with another publishing house. Believing that you were at liberty to do so. Meanwhile the original publishers decided to bring the book out anyway. Without telling you of their intentions. And now there are two identical books on the market."

"Not identical: they have different titles."

"But anyone who saw them both would be in no doubt that they're the same."

"None whatever."

A silence during which George Mascaret imagined the brief gleefully anticipating a case that would stretch out long enough to make Jarndyce and Jarndyce look like a summary hearing for strict liability. He well remembered *Bleak House*: that Tulkinghorn, creepy and bent; no wonder he took a bullet.

"This isn't really my area of expertise but on the face of it I'm struggling to see what damages you've suffered. After all, you've been paid twice for the same piece of work."

"But I may end up looking like I've sold ten thousand per cent of the shares, like in *The Producers*."

A lawyer has few greater pleasures than the chance to show that he's a bit of a cultural all-rounder.

"I loved that film. It's Gene Wilder, isn't it? And Zero Mostel. Directed by Mel Brooks, if I remember rightly."

"Yes."

And then the professional adviser revealed another area of expertise as he put on a stagey Scandiwegian accent:

"'Bialystok and Bloom; Bialystok and Bloom.' That was so funny."

"Yes. My concern is, if I appear untrustworthy, no one will touch me ever again."

"I see the difficulty. It certainly is a most unusual case. I can give you the name of a couple of practices that specialise in intellectual property. I'm sure they'll be extremely interested."

I bet they will, thought George. And by the time their enthusiasm has worn off I'll be sleeping in a cardboard box in the doorway of Freeman Hardy and Willis.

"In the meantime, what I suggest you do is pitch up at this meeting with Skidmore…"

"You mean Volkmer & Iles."

"They're the second ones you approached? The ones who rang you most recently?"

"That's right."

"Yes, present yourself at Volkmer & Iles, as arranged…"

"Like I have a choice."

"Hear what they have to say for themselves. Don't talk; sign nothing; get back to me."

The solicitor added that he wouldn't charge for this meeting because of his long association with the Mascarets. He thought it a kind gesture, the least he could do for a poor struggling artist in society. George thought of his long-dead father, who'd always referred to the man who did the family's conveyancing as the Shoreham Cicero and characterised him as someone who'd take your coat from your back when you arrived in his office and have the shirt off it before you left. But then Mascaret fils reproved himself with the words of Henry de Montherlant: "Charity has no meaning unless it is repaid by hatred" and spent the journey home fretting about where he'd read it.

§

"So what's happening with one-o-one?"

Gill Furneaux wanting a sit rep from her Number Two.

"Not entirely clear, but at the moment it looks like we're going for Skidmore as well as the author."

"Bring it on, the more the merrier. Max wants a blood sacrifice."

"I have to flag a potential complicating factor: Marcus is saying they can prove it's their book; they owned it first."

"That's bullshit, no?"

"Well he couldn't show us a contract, but he says he's got one somewhere. We've given him till tomorrow."

"And if he does produce it?"

"I suppose we join Skidmore in an action against this Masquerade or whatever his name is."

"Keep me in the loop, all right?"

"Sure thing. I'll fill you in later."

Stratton said this the only way he knew.

"Will you indeed."

§

From his quick look at the VI contract Marcus the publisher gleaned a vital datum that he'd either lost or never had: the name of the author. Examining his own bought ledger he discovered that he'd paid this George Mascaret a cool grand a full quarter before the cheating bastard had signed up with the rival house.

The endomorph suggested they ring him, but they couldn't find his number on their decrepit Rolodex. They then agreed that it was prudent to do as little as possible as late as possible and that they should let Volkmer & Iles take the lead. Anyone normal would have been cautiously optimistic, but Marcus's p could equally have stood for paranoiac. He sighed like a punctured bagpipe and droned:

"I still think no formal written agreement, no leg to stand on. Max Volkmer will destroy us without batting a hooded eyelid. Can no one see where this is heading? He'll asset-strip us and close us down. I built up Skidmore single-handed..." Seeing the endomorph look hurt, he corrected himself: "... well, almost single-handed – from nothing. My life's work ruined by a cunt of a writer and admin staff that couldn't organise a fuck at a free brothel."

The endomorph wondered what assets there were, he was damned if he could see any, but he said that if he ever came across Robin Peppiatt he'd shag her senseless and then kill her, an image that cheered them both up so much that they treated themselves to some sport with their commissioning editor, whose reputation was rapidly heading the same way as his predecessor's.

"Coleen, come through. How was your weekend?"

"Good, thanks."

"Where was it you went?"

"St Ives."

That, to Marcus and the endomorph, was even more telling than Brighton.

"Lovely. Now I suppose you're wondering why we've brought you in here."

Colin hadn't been wondering any such thing: meetings like this happened informally several times a day. But come to think of it, the endomorph had just mispronounced his name. No propitious augury. And made a point of closing the door behind him. Definitely a bad sign.

"*Advice to Persons About to Marry.*"

"How's it doing?"

"The reps subscribed a couple of thousand copies."

"That's good, isn't it?"

"Potentially, yes. But there's a glitch."

"Glitch?"

"Yes, glitch. Quite a big one."

They told him what had happened. Colin had no difficulty in expressing – and indeed to some extent feeling – regret but it seemed his interlocutors wanted contrition. That didn't come so easily.

"I have a clear and distinct recollection that you told me all the books on that pile were ours to do with what we liked."

The endomorph snorted.

"You didn't think to double-check?"

"Against what? The records here are not what you'd call comprehensive."

"What on earth possessed you to change the title?"

"I thought it was inspired, much better than the original. You both agreed it."

"But if we'd known what it was we wouldn't have gone ahead in a million years."

Colin said that was wishful thinking: in their moment of crisis they'd have published anything they could get their hands on. Marcus saw that the endomorph's line was too much wisdom after the event. He called off the hunt.

"We've done what we've done. We haven't done what we haven't done. We are where we are. I may be able to swing this but I'm not confident. I want you both to be aware that if I can't get a result when we go back to VI, Skidmore is dead in the water."

§

George Mascaret clung tenaciously to the belief that he'd behaved with exemplary rectitude. He had done no more than any professional writer would have tried to do – sell his work. But just as "the pen is mightier than the sword" looks like wishful thinking late at night in a pub car park when half a dozen Union Jackals confront an effete-looking wit armed only with a poppy or a lily, so even the most rational defence of his conduct would present less of an obstacle to a horde of voracious book peddlers and their legal advisers than Belgium presented to the implementation of the Schlieffen Plan.

On arriving at Volkmer & Iles George was taken to the board room where he was confronted by a man and a woman. The former was about fifty years too young to be the chairman. In a pink shirt with a white collar that looked tight enough to constrict the flow of blood to his brain and an unmatching brown tie, with floppy dyed blond hair swept back behind a widow's peak, this sleaze looked like the actor you might hire if you couldn't afford William Hurt as he appeared in *Body Heat*.

The woman put him in mind of the opening of *Daniel Deronda*. "Was she beautiful or not beautiful?" A stupid question to which the only sensible answer could be "I don't know, Mary Ann; you invented her; you tell me". At least that was how it had always seemed to him until now, when he suddenly recognised the phenomenon to which George Eliot may have been referring – a sexual indeterminateness that was not androgyny (Mascaret saw immediately that Ella was, as they say, all woman) but perhaps an external manifestation of an inner infirmity of eugenic purpose.

That this was no time for internal dialogue about the relations of art to life and of desire to attainment became apparent to George almost right away, from the moment the pair of them set about him like leopards assailing a gormless hartebeest that has become detached from the herd.

The she-cat clawed first:

"When you signed the contract, did you notice section twenty, subsection one, in which 'the author warrants to the publisher that in respect of the text he has full power and authority to make this agreement and this agreement does not infringe the rights or licence of any other person'?"

George Mascaret said that he had. Whether this was an admission or a claim was dubious, however, because he hadn't read the whole of the document, or at least if he had he hadn't taken any of it in apart from the money on offer. But he couldn't deny that he'd signed it.

"And did you also notice subsection two: 'The author is the sole author of the text which is original and has not been published in any form'?"

Another affirmation. Now the spotty male pounced.

"In that case, I have to tell you that we will be pursuing you for every penny that we have spent on this book – your advance, the printing costs, the paper, the promotion and distribution. We will also be seeking punitive damages."

Although frightened, George knew that this was a response which might be described as sound and fury by those who'd read Shakespeare or as piss and wind by anyone who had not been educated out of his wits and whose first line of defence was not always a quotation, apposite or not. Even if they decided to pursue this course, they'd be unlikely to collect because he didn't have the money. But George didn't want a fight because a fight would attract bad publicity and bad publicity would damage his reputation. Whatever that was. A minuscule bubble. But bubbles can fly high before they succumb to the inevitable. He abandoned the path mapped out for him by Tulkinghorn.

"Wait," he said. "Listen. I can explain everything."

§

Half an hour into her three o'clock meeting at the Heathrow hotel, the managing director of Volkmer & Iles lay on the floor wearing only a cheese-cutter thong while the firm's marketing director sat naked in an armchair with legs crossed conceitedly smoking a cigarette.

As planes landed outside the window, he reported what George Mascaret had told Jake and Ella.

"Circumstances alter cases. We will gain nothing from sticking writs on some penniless hack and a firm that looks for all the world like it's trading while insolvent."

"We can't let this go unpunished. If the press get hold of it we're in deep shit, especially after *The* fucking *Catcher in the Rye*."

"Let me tell you a story."

"Is it long?"

"Not very."

"Is it dull?"

"Decide for yourself. When I was learning Spanish I came across this fable about two little boys."

Gill sang the last three words in the hit single version by Rolf Harris. Baxter ignored her so she added "had two little toys". Still no response.

"Two little boys are playing underneath a tree when a walnut drops off it and falls in front of them. The first boy says 'It's mine, I saw it first'. The second boy says 'No, no, it's mine, it landed closer to me'. They start fighting. Along comes a man. He pulls them apart. 'What are you fighting about?' the man asks…"

"You're a loss to stand-up, Baxter Stratton."

"So the boys tell him the story so far…"

"I feel this could do with a bit of polishing…"

"The man gets hold of the nut, cracks it, and says to them: 'I am going to bring you to an agreement'. He then gives half of the shell to the first boy and the other half of the shell to the second boy. Then he says: 'As for the kernel, I am keeping that for myself as payment for the decision I have given'. And then he puts it in his mouth and as he chews it he laughs and says *'Este es el resultado de todos los pleitos'* – 'This is the result of all law suits'."

"Highly illustrative. So we waste some money. It won't be the first time. Max is concerned that we'll look foolish; we need to go through the motions."

"I've got a better idea. We can pull a flanker."

He told her what he had in mind.

Gill walked over to the chair and sat on top of him.

"This is the only way I'd ever turn my back on you."

"You mean we're together forever?"

"God I hope not."

"You mean you don't trust me?"

"Only to be devious."

"I'm a businessman."

"Don't be ridiculous… oof… You're forty-five and in publishing. The smartest people never got into books in the first place; the best of the rest realised their mistake early and got out after a couple of years… ooh, yes."

"What's your… excuse?"

"Events, dear boy, events. Marriage. I'm good at what I do… but I've also… profited… from tokenism… a bird… Max… Volkmer put… on… a high… perch… as a decoy… to fool… other women… into thinking there's… no… glass… ceil-iiiiiing…"

§

George Mascaret grabbed an hour of quiet after passion. Not postcoital as described by Macneice in "Trilogy for X" but postproelial. He couldn't claim victory, but he felt that, having spoken with unwonted cogency, he had come out with an honourable draw, that the struggle had nought-nought availeth.

How different this day from most of his others, which had been characterised by either saying too little, which he identified as Cordelia syndrome, or too much, which he thought should become known to medical science as Mascaret's chorea. He didn't know what had inspired him to the heights of rhetoric he'd attained in the board room, but he wondered if it might have been the blow dealt to his pride by Max Volkmer's absence from the meeting: acting on instructions from Gill Furneaux, Ella had invoked the chairman's name merely in order to ensure that George was made fully aware of the seriousness of his predicament.

Back at his desk before Vivienne and the children got home, George had another go at *Don Quixote*. Chapter Six – five and a half pages "Of the diverting and minute scrutiny performed by the curate and the barber, in the library of our sagacious hero" – took him longer to read than no doubt Cervantes to write and Smollett to translate put together. He wrote in his Journal the heading "Pilate Training: How Pontius won promotion from Flight Sergeant". Beneath it he put:

"What is Truth?"

and then on a new line below:

"It is easier to buy a book than to read one".

Having found on his return no letter from Wilby Bestsellers, who still owed him for the joke diptych, he added:

"It is easier to generate an invoice than to bank a cheque."

And then he thought: when you consider the events throughout human history that must all occur in order to make possible your existence – your parents have to conceive, not just with each other but at a certain moment, and the same goes for all their ancestors back to the Big Bang – why should the same sequence not one day recur? Just as there is no reason why the same six numbers plus the bonus should not come up on more than one occasion in the lottery. Unlikely, no doubt, but not impossible. When you further consider the difficulties of getting your work into print.... Finding a publisher may be accounted a near miracle; to get the same book into shops twice at almost the same time may be even more philosophically and spiritually significant: taken together, *101 Reasons for Staying Single* and *Advice to Persons About to Marry* are evidence of the possibility of reincarnation.

But he didn't write any of that down because he thought it would look mental.

§

If Ella had had anyone to confide in, she'd have told her (or, perhaps preferably, him) that she was on the point of resigning.

And he or she would have scorned the idea and said that people who really are about to do something momentous don't talk, they just get on with it.

To which Ella's response would have been that she had always wanted to indulge and capitalise on her love of literature. And that when she had accepted her current job she thought she'd finally achieved her life's ambition. But talk about "Beware lest your dreams come true": it took her nearly half a year to get any of her selections taken up, and thereafter everything that she approved became a road wreck.

Her friend the sounding board might then have reminded her that she hadn't accepted anything; she'd been instructed to take on additional responsibility. The only choice she had been given was that between liking it and putting up with it. Her new job began as an honour without profit; although VI had subsequently agreed to pay her a finder's fee, the amount per book was so small as to be scarcely worth mentioning. Which was just as well, because she had never been paid one and now there was so much debris lying around her that she was scared of reminding them.

The unkindest cut was the realisation that her judgment, though dependable in aesthetic terms (she thought of all the manuscripts she'd rejected and regretted none of them), was less valuable than the interwar Reichsmark.

By the time Ella reached this conclusion, she had admitted to herself the possibility that her attraction to cheats must be more powerful than she had previously realised. Take Jake. Yes, take him. A CAUC indeed. And the fantasist Hoffmann, who'd held her spellbound over the North Sea before dropping her in it. And now Mascaret, who had seemed almost like a proper writer on the page but turned out to be a fraud, no better than any of the rest of them. She'd noticed him eyeing her up during their meeting: what kind of a man would do that when his whole livelihood was on the line? Is that all men ever think about? Women's magazines seemed unanimous that it was, but in her experience – which was less extensive than a part of her would have liked – she had nearly always been the one who did the kissing, her lovers the ones who proffered their cheeks.

§

Marcus the publisher surveyed the Volkmer & Iles building with an enthusiasm similar to that no doubt felt by woodcutters on first descrying a castle on a rocky promontory in the heart of Transylvania.

With him, instead of crucifix and garlic, he brought Colin

Dodd and the endomorph. Although he regarded them as less use than, respectively or not, male nipples and the Pope's penis, he wanted disciples to accompany him along the Via Dolorosa and witness his martyrdom. They too were nervous, but they weren't bricking it like their boss: to them, Skidmore was just an employer; to Marcus, it was the be-all that was just about to all end.

In the VI board room the Skidmores were outnumbered two to one. Lined up on the other side of the table were Max Volkmer, Gill Furneaux, Baxter Stratton, Willie Lechler, Jacob Pursey and Tim Etchells, the one known as Eenie.

Marcus had decided that he'd not go down without a fight. Removing some photocopies from a plastic folder he launched straight in with:

"Now I'm afraid that our contract with George Mascaret is confidential and I am not prepared to divulge it to you, but I can disclose this, the record of our initial payment to him. As you will see, it antedates your agreement by a considerable period of time."

The document was passed around.

"In the light of that", Marcus the publisher continued when they'd all had a chance to look at it, "it would appear that if anyone is going to have to pulp a book it isn't going to be Skidmore".

Max Volkmer broke the ensuing silence.

"Mr Skidmore, may I call you Marcus?"

M the p braced himself for impact.

"I fear there may have been a misunderstanding. Our two houses are both alike in dignity. We are by no means suggesting that you should destroy your book, any more than we would contemplate withdrawing ours. The way forward is, I think, perfectly clear."

M the p realised that the collision was not about to be head-on. That was something of a relief but he remained suspicious of Max's insouciance. It was like a nightmare in which escapes lead to worse trouble: but from which direction was the next stroke going to come?

Max Volkmer then proceeded to pass off Baxter Stratton's big idea as his own.

Chapter Six: Prose and Cons

On a slow day at VI, Gill Furneaux and Baxter Stratton were out of the office, severally or together, no one knew or much cared which. Jacob Pursey was passing through reception on his way back from lunch with a prospective author when every one of the red lights on the switchboard console started flashing simultaneously.

To the first three callers the receptionist said: "I'll just put you through"; to the rest she said, "Lines are busy: do you want to hold?"

On emerging a minute later from the lift, Pursey was confronted by his normally torpid sales department in a paroxysm of previously unimagined bustle. The place looked for once more like a newsroom than a Hopper painting. Asking what gave, he learned that Clarissa Newnham had been shortlisted for the Booker Prize and that every bookseller in the realm was after dumpbins full of *Behind A Dream.*

He took a couple of calls himself, scribbling down the orders on the margins of his *Evening Standard.* Then, shutting out the activity around him, he stuck his finger through the hanger of the jacket that he'd left strategically on the back of his chair during his long absence, slung it over his shoulder, dropped the newspaper on the desk of some marketing assistant to whom he'd have been pushed to put a name and left for the day. It was a quarter past four. Pursey decided that he really needed to put his father right about one of the precepts. Number six really had no relevance to his working life: he never worked late, and no matter how early he knocked off his bosses had gone already.

Strolling to the car park he reflected on all the time he'd wasted touting books that were published merely to service an overhead: VI exists and has offices and staff, therefore it must bring out books. And on the humiliations of trying to flog titles that customers didn't want but which they might be persuaded to take on sale or return. He recalled in particular an occasion not long after he'd become sales manager when he'd offered some wholesalers an extra five per cent discount if they'd double the quantities. The response had been: "Are you that desperate?" How much easier it was to sell a product that was actually in demand.

§

Whether through editorial discernment, penetrative marketing, blind chance or a combination of two or all three of those ingredients, other books on VI's frontlist were doing well too. Foremost among them was *101 Reasons for Staying Single*.

Max Volkmer and Marcus the publisher had demanded that everyone in the meeting keep quiet about their agreement. Nevertheless or consequently, the story set a new record time for six laps of the book trade.

The press and broadcast media must have got hold of the story in outline at least, but they showed no interest in covering it. Perhaps they didn't understand or thought it would take too much explaining or be too complicated for their audience. Maybe they figured that most people would remark nothing odd at all. Only the most observant would notice the anomalies: that VI and Skidmore were unconnected (neither was an imprint of the other); that the books, despite their different titles, were textually identical; that the limp edition cost more than the cased.

Gill Furneaux and Baxter Stratton had no difficulty in identifying the snitch, the whistleblower to their own complete satisfaction. Willie Lechler had tried to sabotage *101 Reasons* out of spite because he'd had no part in it. In just the same way as he'd shafted *Roosevelt's Secret Agent*. And as he'd grassed Jake Pursey up to *Private Eye*. Being of one mind that it would be better to have Willie outside the tent, regardless of the direction in which he was pissing, they considered firing him for gross misconduct, but decided against because the leak could just as easily have come from a bookseller or a reader. Anyway, Willie's presumed perfidy fitted in well with the overall plan: they wanted the story to spread, and insofar as it is possible to guarantee such an outcome, the best way is to tell a very few people, carefully chosen for their indiscretion, that it's top secret.

More likely Willie was too stoical for malice; he merely wanted to demonstrate the lack of wisdom with which the world is run. Yet whatever his motives, his loose tongue had exactly the opposite of the anticipated effect, which was that both books would flop; he could not have made a worse miscalculation of the behaviour of the market.

Across town, *Advice to Persons About to Marry* was exceeding even the most optimistic forecasts. Staff at Skidmore were never upbeat about anything, so the prediction bar had not been set very high; still there was no denying the evidence of the printouts. The outstanding feature of the book's success was that, according to reports coming in-house from shops via the reps, sales were inextricably linked to those of *101 Reasons for Staying Single*: customers bought both of them together in what it amused Marcus to call one swell foop.

This was just as Baxter Stratton had predicted: that the two books, humiliating though they were for Skidmore, VI and the author, would become valuable curiosities that were snapped up and cherished by bibliophiles and students of the pathology of publishing. Gill Furneaux relayed this prognostication to Max Volkmer, mutatis mutandis of course to pass it off as her own. The chairman then appropriated it on the grounds that only he had the clout to get it across to the Skidmore three. When it was put to Marcus the publisher, he saw its merit immediately; even if he hadn't seen it he had no alternative, so he agreed unhesitatingly, enthusiastically even. And Colin and the endomorph nodded vigorously because that was what they were paid to do.

But sometimes the trouble with a brilliant idea is that people spend so long thinking of ways in which it might not work that they fail to see the problems that may arise if it does. What they missed here was the possibility that one book would sell out before the other. Since Skidmore had printed only half as many copies of *Advice* as VI had produced of *101*, that, just over a month later, was exactly what happened.

With no cash reserves, Marcus the publisher asked VI if they might like to subsidise his reprint. Stratton scoffed at the suggestion, so anyone who tried to order the Skidmore book after the middle of October got the response "reprint under consideration (no date)" that those in the know took to mean "never".

§

Ella Bethune had tried with Clarissa Newnham at numerous launch parties and sales conferences but always found her incoherently drunk. Or at least, pretending to be. That was probably more like it. The great author either had the capacity for alcohol of a twelve-year-old or else her reeling and a-slurring were the salient defences of a woman who didn't really like social events. And who could blame her for despising convocations of commercial toadies and earnest book buyers who told her they had found in her work the influence of writers she'd scarcely heard of, let alone read?

Problems such as this are universal and commonplace and therefore dull. What's interesting is the solutions. Especially if they're bravura. The best that could be said for Clarissa

Newnham's method of dealing with her inhibitions was that it lacked kindliness.

The first time they met, Ella made a point of keeping the talk small. A bit about the current parlous state of public transport, a nod in the direction of the weather, an expression of mild surprise that the Liberal Party was about to ditch another leader. And then, thinking she detected a bit of a thaw in Clarissa, she threw in a casual one about the paucity of eligible men in the room. This broke the ice, all right, but got her only as far as the cold water underneath. Clarissa advised her to grab a husband quick lest she be left on the shelf.

At the start of a subsequent encounter, Clarissa claimed she well remembered Ella but hadn't recognised her because she'd put on so much weight. Which as a matter of fact she hadn't, but that wasn't the point. The point was that Clarissa Newnham wished not to be there; since that objective had proved unattainable she was going to do everything in her power to get the others present to bugger off and leave her be.

On Booker night, Ella watched the award dinner on telly home alone with a takeaway. As the cameras raked around the Guildhall she got frequent glimpses of the VI table: Max Volkmer fressing like a famished wolf, peering around furtively as if in fear that someone might snatch his food away from him; on his left, Harold Iles, looking too old for the Politburo; on his right, Gill Furneaux, who though expensively dressed for the nonce still looked as she did in her workaday rig – a woman who made up for her looks with an aura of availability. Also present were the novelist herself, who put Ella in mind of late-period Henry VIII, albeit without the beard, and Vernon Kanzell in white deejay and multicoloured waistcoat. Next to the agent was Baxter Stratton, whose on-screen appearance was almost indistinguishable from the oleaginous reality: fairly suave, entirely heartless and oddly not quite all there, as if he had stood in at short notice for a late cancellation. Ella was not surprised by the absence of Willie Lechler: editorial director or not, he was in the outer darkness. Although she hadn't expected to see Jacob Pursey there either, she felt oddly sorry that he hadn't had the pick. There was nothing he'd have liked more – she knew that because he'd spent weeks telling her that he thought he ought to be invited. She believed that, in general, if people want something badly enough to ask for it they should be given it at once.

The prize was awarded to Solveig Rawtenstall. After her acceptance speech, the coverage returned to the studio where a guest pundit said he wasn't altogether surprised that *Behind A Dream* had failed to win, because it was the work of a woman *d'un certain âge* who needed to stop pretending she was a little girl. Ella grunted semi-approval through a half-chewed wedge of Veneziana pizza.

§

Jez Yaxley dreaded all calls from authors, but this one was more than usually unwelcome.

"Hi, George, good to hear from you."

He was about to add "How's it hanging?" but managed to change the last word to "going" fluently enough to make it seem as if that was the word he'd intended from the off.

"Not too shabby, as my children would say. You?"

"Mustn't… er… rage too much against the machine."

"Good, good. I was just wondering what happened about the joke book."

"Aah, the joke book. I've been meaning to ring you. The trouble is that we had a lot of difficulty finding an acceptable quote. The costs of making a book in that quite particular shape were much higher than we'd anticipated. Eventually we found printers in Taiwan who were cheap enough, but unfortunately they couldn't do it."

"A printer turns down business? What kind of a world are we living in?"

"Well, to be perfectly frank, it wasn't so much couldn't as wouldn't. The fact is they rejected it on moral grounds."

"Oh. That's a shame."

"That's almost exactly what they said. Or maybe it was 'shameful'."

George laughed perfunctorily.

"Anyway, you've probably gone past caring now, what with at least two best-selling books on your slate. Congratulations."

"Why, I thank you, but you must know there's a difference between a best-seller and a book that makes the author any money."

"Were you on a flat fee for both of them?"

"No, only for the Skidmore one, *Advice to Persons About to Marry. 101 Reasons for Staying Single* was a royalty deal, but Volkmer & Iles remaindered it straight after Christmas. They offered me four thousand copies at ten pee each."

"So are you surrounded by them as we speak?"

George thought of essaying some mot about the Fifth Amendment, but before he could think of one another quotation popped out:

"Sufficient unto the day is the evil thereof".

He wasn't sure how appropriate or relevant this was in context, and doubted that Jez would get what he meant.

But he did.

"You mean you bought them?"

No coherent reply; just a noise that was part grunt, part groan.

"All? Oh, Jesus."

After he'd hung up, Jez Yaxley made wankers at the phone and then flicked a few V's at it for good measure.

§

When Colin Dodd announced that he'd be leaving Skidmore at the end of the month, the endomorph struggled to conceal his delight: the fewer his colleagues, the safer his own position.

Less happy, Marcus the publisher told Colin that the book trade was a small world, very small. He said he hoped that when they met again, at wayzgooses, on working parties, wherever, they'd be able to greet each other cordially, compare success stories and share happy memories of their time together, but warned him that, unfortunately, that would not be possible if he insisted on going before he'd worked a full three months' notice.

With no mortgage, no girl friend or boy friend, and no prospects other than an endless succession of thankless editorial tasks intercalated only by occasional cheap lunches with authors and Christmas parties at the local Indian where the bosses made great show of not calling the waiter Gunga Din, Colin could reasonably have asked if there was any possibility that Marcus was confusing him with someone who gave a fuck about any of that.

But he replied emolliently that he could not go on beyond the thirtieth because he had booked a flight to Los Angeles for first thing the following morning. The start of his round-the-world trip.

Marcus wanted to say "That's not my fault; unbook it" but he knew that, given the iniquities of employment law, he could not keep the monkey tethered against its will. And an uppity slave is worse than no slave at all. So he wished him well, or said he did.

They had no further contact until leaving day, when Colin Dodd dared to be different and joined his bosses for a sesh at The Albion.

Marcus the publisher drank to forget, which seemed ludicrous in view of his struggles to remember anything when

he was sober. With the guest of honour away from the table –
"breaking the seal", they called it – he leaned over to the
endomorph and said:

"You know, anyone who leaves Skidmore now is admitting
defeat."

"Just as the company really starts to take off."

"Exactly."

"He's a silly arse, isn't he?"

"You can say that again."

"He's a silly arse."

"Are you looking for a replacement?"

"I don't know. We haven't had a lot of luck with editors,
have we? First that silly little bird, now this one. Do you think
we need to?"

"I think we could do without for a while; it'd give us a
leaner, meaner, more streamlined machine."

"It'll be a lot more on your plate."

"I haven't got a problem with that. I've been doing the
work of at least two people for quite a while now."

"I know. You're a sound fellow. What went wrong with
him? He seemed all right for a while. He was almost good, he
was getting there."

"He wanted more top-end involvement. And when he
didn't get it he turned bloody-minded. His problem is loads of
ambition and not much ability, a lethal combination."

"I think you're right. In fact I think you're pretty well
always right. I like that. Good instincts."

After three more pints each, they returned to the office for the presentation of a valedictory card and twenty pounds' worth of book tokens.

Marcus made a short speech.

"Well, Colin, this is it. Goodbye. Things won't be the same without you. I won't say whether they'll be better or worse."

Everyone laughed the way they laugh at undertakers.

"Is anyone here old enough to remember *Z-Cars*? BBC cop series of the nineteen sixties. Set in Liverpool. No response; no matter. They still play the theme tune to it at Everton when the teams come out. Not that any of you know that, most probably. I have to say that didn't myself until I read our acclaimed book of footie songs, four ninety-five, available to staff at a most generous fifty per cent discount. Don't let me discourage you from buying multiple copies. It's about a sailor called Johnny Todd. Johnny Todd, Colin Dodd, you see, same sort of thing, not much difference to speak of. I won't sing it, you'll be relieved to hear, but the words are, or could be:

'Colin Dodd he took a notion

For to cross the ocean wide

And he left Skidmore behind him

Thriving on the English side.'

"Anyway, Johnny, Colin, Todd, Dodd, sod, whatever your name is, thank you for your contribution. Shame it couldn't have been more. Enjoy the world. Arrivederci."

And so saying Marcus the publisher slumped into the nearest chair.

§

George Mascaret worried that the double booking would make publishers regard him as unusable: what he had done, or seemed to have done, looked like sharp practice. He imagined "2H2H" ("too hot to handle") being written beside his name on lists of possible contributors all over the English-speaking world.

But his fears were unfounded; still the work came in, not in battalions, nor yet in single spies but in something in between, a steady enough trickle to keep him liquid.

In spring The Clifford Press sent him a headword list of articles that still needed writing for *The Fina A–Z of Literary Forms*, volumes E–K, L–R and S–Z. Ciaran Addey told him he could have any one he liked. Evidently George's misdemeanour on the cricket field had also been forgiven – or more likely forgotten.

The topics that appealed to him – foremost among which were "Satire" and "Verse Drama" – had been crossed out, having already been taken by lecturers at new universities in Britain and colleges in the United States. No doubt if George played his cards right he would in due course get several of them to "edit". It ain't stealin'.

He was left with a choice of dregs. Some were beyond his competence: "The Gothic Novel"; "Magical Realism"; "Pamphlets and Tracts". Others were either too boring or too much like hard work to contemplate, especially for the fee on offer: "The Objective Correlative" (Eliot: so long dead yet still as inescapable as he'd been in life); "The Pathetic Fallacy" (please, no); "The Picaresque" (more Smollett? Not in this incarnation).

Eventually he plumped for five thousand words on "The Sonnet". As he was writing his mind kept wandering onto one of the subjects he'd fancied but which had already been assigned: "Endings".

About them he had much to say, although he realised that was a compelling reason for him not to write the article: the stronger one's views, the harder to achieve the "style neutral" that publishers want in works of this kind.

He began at the beginning – no in medias res for him. A couple of paragraphs about the sonnet form before it found its way into English: the Provençal troubadours, the poets of Norman Sicily. And thence to Florence and a long section on Petrarch.

He recalled Wilde: "The good ended happily, and the bad unhappily. That is what fiction means". Then E.M. Forster: "If it was not for death and marriage I do not know how the average novelist would conclude. Nearly all novels are feeble at the end".

And so they are. Feeble. Certainly those that George had finished (which were not many, mainly set books). Still, if Forster had been there before him, there was no need for him to bother repeating the experiment for the sake of saying he'd done so. After all, unless you take copious notes, all you remember about most books a month after you've finished them is whether they were good (one or two) or crap (the majority). In sum, Morgan mate, he thought, I'm prepared to take your word for it.

That being the case, was it true to say that, in that particular, the ends of novels were mirroring the approach to death, "… last stage of all,/When we are frozen up within, and quite/The phantom of ourselves", setra setra? Or were they mere contrivances, "with one bound he was free"s, emergency exits through which authors and readers could slip back into the daylight and get on with their lives?

Then he wrote about Wyatt and Surrey, the sixteenth-century import firm that shipped in strong Italian produce and diluted it to English taste. He worked in a sonorous quotation from Legouis's and Cazamian's *History of English Literature* that had the double benefit of giving his piece authority and filling a couple of dozen words of his quota.

Come to think of it, George thought, it wasn't only novels that were unsatisfactory at the end. The only pieces of music that struck him as properly resolved, with all the loose ends pleasingly bowed up, were The Waltz of the Flowers in *The Nutcracker* and Schubert's String Quintet in C. But he didn't know enough about the subject to adduce any supporting evidence. So it was just an opinion, and opinions were cheap, everyone had them. What people didn't have was knowledge; and that, he thought, was where he came in.

Philip Sidney and Samuel Daniel were pointed out like landmarks on a tour, announced like stations on the line to

Michael Drayton, now visible from the windows on either side of the carriage.

George recalled a book of his nonage, possibly an Enid Blyton, in which the good children were rewarded with a magic hardback that added an extra page every time they reached what had been the end. The beneficiaries were described as having been delighted, but it seemed to him like the kind of curse gift that would have made King Midas count his blessings.

And then the trippers stopped for lunch at William Shakespeare, with a chance to glimpse through a translucent screen the shadowy outline of the Dark Lady. Or was it the dark bloke? A fascinating question that we won't be dealing with in detail or indeed at all. We must move on now to look around two of our greatest ecclesiastical structures, Donne and Milton.

Writers contrive resolutions for situations that in real life would have none. Most fictional characters would carry on after the curtain falls in much the same way as they had while the lights were down. Relationships may end with a bang, but more commonly they slip away beneath the horizon, diminuendo in endless microscopic divisions that cannot be replicated or evoked on the page. Of course, an author can always kill his characters but often there's no concealing that death in art is more endgame than Truth; it is seldom convincing even as an imitation of an action.

And then the itinerary took sonnet-seekers through Hampstead for a look at Keats. Aah, Keats, who claimed in an ode that he felt as if he'd drunk of Lethe, but he couldn't have had the faintest idea what that was really like…. So if the second or third greatest poet in the English language was just a chancer, where did that leave the rest of them?

There followed a dash to the Lake District for Wordsworth and then back to London for a short time with the token woman, Elizabeth Barrett Browning. And that, apart from a nod in the direction of Dante Gabriel Rossetti, was about all there was to it. George Mascaret then knocked off a pithy peroration that would no doubt be dropped by Ciaran Addey into the same bin as that into which he had slung "nugatory".

Finally, triumphally though otiosely, because encyclopedia entries never finish this way, he put at the bottom:

THE END

but he crossed it out before he went to bed.

§

Six months later, this appeared in a national Sunday newspaper under the byline of the author of *Croak Monsieur.*
"The Spy Who Stayed Out in the Cold
"If you want a fictional old lady who solves mysteries, you need look no further than Agatha Christie's Miss Marple. If you want a real old lady whose whole life is a mystery, you can do no better than spend an afternoon in the company of Jan Hoffmann.

"A white-haired American, Ms Hoffmann insists that she was a spy who worked for U.S. President Franklin D. Roosevelt and led a secret mission to assassinate Vidkun Quisling, the puppet leader of Nazi-occupied Norway.

"She claims to be 90. She's a very sprightly 90, but that's not why I say, 'claims to be'. The problem with Ms Hoffmann is that no one knows what to believe.

"I met her in Manhattan's Algonquin Hotel, once the hangout of Dorothy Parker and her Vicious Circle.

"Publisher Volkmer & Iles was on the point of bringing out her memoirs: jackets were printed, press adverts booked, foreign editions sold, a publicity tour lined up, the whole shebang.

"And then, without warning, the book was cancelled. Shortage of funds or crisis of confidence? Officially Volkmer & Iles would not say. But privately senior executives spoke of several claims in the book that no one could verify and many more about which experts have expressed grave doubts, none graver than over Hoffmann's assertion that Roosevelt wanted the Soviet Union to get the nuclear bomb. Nonsense, say professional historians.

"When I put these misgivings to Ms Hoffmann, she is quite unfazed: she has after all heard them many times before. She tells me that her cover was so deep that even now she is not free to break it completely. Much of what she heard and did during the War was so secret that it was never written down.

"According to her, the proof is in the handwritten letter from FDR, which she shows me proudly. But this too has been rubbished, not only by graphologists but also by the President's biographers.

"When I mention this, Ms Hoffmann responds with a long, hard stare: 'The President wrote that letter in front of me. He knew there would be doubters. This was my get-out-of-jail-free card'.

"Some people think that Jan Hoffmann is like Winston Churchill's Russia: a riddle, wrapped in a mystery, inside an enigma. Others think she is a Walter Mitty.

"But a stalwart few have stuck firmly by her. Currently the foremost of her supporters is publisher Ross Runnacles who, hearing that Volkmer & Iles had iced the book, stepped into the breach and is bringing it out under his own new Bristol-based imprint. Now you can read Jan Hoffmann's amazing story and judge for yourself if she's telling the truth.

"*Roosevelt's Secret Agent: The Book They Tried To Ban* is published next Thursday by RR Editions at £9.99."

"What do you make of that then?" asked Jacob Pursey when Ella Bethune had finished reading.

"I don't know. I've decided that I really don't understand anything much. Everything I do turns out entirely unexpectedly. Maybe I should make up my mind what's right and then do the exact opposite."

"You seem very down."

"Do I?"

"Yes, a bit. How about dinner tonight, let me cheer you up?"

"Okay, then, Jake; might as well; why not?"

WriteSideLeft
2020

www.writesideleft.com

www.ingramcontent.com/pod-product-compliance
Lightning Source LLC
Chambersburg PA
CBHW030625190726
48286CB00008B/2402